Z263-A

A Galactic Honeymoon

Don Hayward

Hey sky, take off your hat, I'm on my way!
- Valentina Tereshkova

ISBN: 9781738064120 (Softcover)

Published 2025 by **DHP**
8 Huron Lane, Goderich, Ontario, Canada N7A 3Y2

Cover photo: Photovision, Pixaby.com

Also by Don Hayward

Collapse
Book One of After the Last Day
ISBN 9781775245926 (Soft cover)

Under Shadows
Book Two of After the last Day
ISBN 9781775245940 (Softcover)

The End of shadows
Book Three of After the Last Day
ISBN 9781775245957 (Soft cover)

The Seventh Path
ISBN 9781621379492 (Soft cover)

Journey's End
ISBN 9781775245933 (Soft cover)

Murder on the Goderich Local
ISBN 9781621379935 (Soft cover)

Sherwood Green
ISBN 9781775245902 (Soft cover)

Return
ISBN 9781775245971 (Soft cover)

Echo of the Whip-poor-will
ISBN 9781775245919 (Soft cover)

High Falls
A pictorial history
ISBN 9781775245964 (Soft cover)

All of Don's books, except High Falls, are available in an electronic version from Smashwords.com, other on-line booksellers.
Most books are available through booksellers worldwide.

Contact Don,
haywardon@gmail.com
https://danddhayward.ca/index.html

The quantum multi-verse is in everyone's heads. Writers just open the doors.

Dedication

To everyone who dreams of the stars and struggles for a better Earth.

Chapter 1

Space

For small creatures such as us, the vastness is bearable only through love. - Carl Sagan

"The void is the enemy," Siglinde said, "the infinite vacuum with no life, no love."

When did I become a poet? She asked herself.

The vast emptiness had a few bright dots and the distant smudge of a local galaxy. She turned away from the view port and to her alien lover, now as a human, astrophysicist Adonis. At least, Siglinde saw Ted, her love in his human form, as the "hot hunk" that her anthropologist friend Liz described.

Of course, Ted was much more; he was an alien mind that held the quantum understanding that he could not share with Siglinde who merely had a human brain, although her brain certainly demanded admiration. The desire for that alien knowledge added to her lust and love.

This new world of emotion and giddiness proved to be a comfortable place to Siglinde, the normal, matter-of-fact physicist. Still, it seemed as alien as the craft that carried her to an even more mysterious world, Z263-A.

The events of the past few months, aliens on Earth, en-mass, and the revelation that her love, Ted, was a star traveller, had collapsed the un-certainty of her life of theory and analysis. Siglinde felt it transformed her from experimenter to the experiment, a quantum speck in fuzzy orbit about a mysterious reality.

"Strange," Ted took her hand, "star travellers see the quantum soup, roiling, threatening, but one that also promises life. We opened the box and found the living universe. Look again..."

Siglinde turned; stars spread beneath her feet. Ted had adjusted the viewing port with his mind to allow through the greater galactic brilliance beneath the ship. Siglinde had experienced a same feeling of hanging in nothingness on a glass-floored tourist walkway that protruded over a cliff high above the Athabasca River. Then the river tumbled far below and roared between steep canyon walls. Thick, coniferous forest swept up the valley slope to the barren talus fields, and jagged peaks soared skyward high above. The ship arched above the galactic plane where the galaxy dominated the dark infinity.

"I forgot how visual humans are." Ted's lips found her cheek. Siglinde sighed and slumped against her love.

The best planetariums on Earth used the latest three-dimensional computer techniques to immerse the audience in a realistic simulation of a trip such as this actual one that carried Siglinde to the stars. Ted had helped a school friend develop such a programme that approached science fiction holodeck realism. Siglinde wondered if the technology had not come from alien ability and not human ingenuity. In her new vision of the future, she did not care. She simply understood that if alien technology became available to humans, it would be as if they had given a child a loaded gun. The evidence on Earth showed that would lead to disaster, and the human population would have to reach the equivalent of the galactic age-of-majority to be trusted with any of that power. Aliens on Earth seemed to be galactic doorkeepers checking human I.D.

She sighed at the enormity of the problem, and the likelihood that humanity would fail, admission denied.

"Where is Z263-A?" Siglinde asked.

"That one," Ted pointed to a faint dot beside Siglinde's right foot near the lower edge of the frame. The yellow star projected mystery and reinforced Siglinde's curiosity about their target, Z263-A, the moon-planet Jewel.

"We are following a gravitational arc slightly above the spiral plane," Ted said, "and will drop to it in three days, your Earth days anyway."

"Your gravitational manipulations, demonstrating base energy and type-1 energy, have bothered me since RoH described it and showed by levitating me."

"RoH sort of simplified it." Ted said and laughed. "It was a good show we all enjoyed."

"Yes, the RoH show" Siglinde said, "RoH said she gave me the Grade 3 version. I'm glad I didn't know you all laughed at me."

"Few laughed," Ted frowned. "We lost humour millennia ago. RoH insists we need to have it again. My life on Earth makes me agree. She keeps trying to make us laugh.

"What is your question?" Ted asked.

"Acceleration in space, in human understanding, every part of our body should feel that force and be affected. In rocket launches, a person normally feels about three times the force of gravity and our faces distort and so forth. I did not experience that when RoH played her game, and I don't feel it on the ship. It's why I couldn't tell when she actually moved me from when she just tricked my brain into thinking I had moved. Why is that?"

"Imagine our bodies are a reference frame, and also this ship." Ted said. "Every baryon in the frame experiences the same acceleration and therefore their relationship to each other does not change. You don't get a launch monkey-face. When we accelerate a frame like this ship into the quantum void of base energy, every baryon inside the follows into its void. It's not like a rocket motor pushing us."

"According to Einstein," Siglinde said, "we should experience time dilation. Does that mean Earth, and perhaps Jewel, are both aging faster than I am on the ship?"

"No," Ted said, "time is not a dimension, as your scientists and fiction writers like to describe it. The universal arrow of time is simply the energy transformations of the entropy of Type 1 or baryonic energy, or the reverse if it can be done. Time scales are artificial units applied to track the order of these energy transformations. If we reversed entropy and concentrated energy, time measurement would look the same and seem to pass in the same direction. Say when we boil water, we measure the time it takes for the concentration of energy in the water to boil it, reverse entropy as far as the water is concerned. Then, if we let the hot water sit and cool, let the energy disperse in entropy, our clock still goes in the same direction. The energy is lost to the air and not back into the heating element. Time did not reverse. The information, order of energy, in the heating element is lost forever. Time travel is not possible. Sadly, there is no future or past Siglinde for me to love."

Ted kissed her.

"Every time measuring scale uses some base energy transformation, the swing of a pendulum or the energy shifts in an atom to define time units. As Einstein described, the frame of reference defines the rate of these changes relative to other frames. Within each frame, time seems to be normal because all energy transformations within the frame are relative. Nothing accelerates, so Einstein's transformation does not apply. We age on the ship at the same rate as on Earth."

"Don't we age less than on Earth?"

"If we were still in Earth's continuum, yes, but we are not. The ship, and all of us, is a bit of Type 1 energy pinched off from the continuum, the Base energy universe, and in a void that is neither the continuum nor the baryonic, that is Earth or Jewel frame of the continuum. Inside this bubble, we are moving in a void in Base Energy, just like Earth is doing at lower speed. Our apparent velocity relative to the universe is simply Base Energy dragging us along trying to fill the artificial void we created in the base."

"How fast are we moving? Is there a limit?"

"There seems to be no theoretical limit, but in practice we cannot generate a perfect void. The strength of our quantum generators, that is our mechanically enhanced minds, decides how good the void is. So far, our speed record is just over eleven hundred times the speed of Type 1 light in a vacuum. This ship is close to that, with five minds in the control loop. We are testing designs with up to ten entities in the seats, but the velocity gain seems to be so slight that it isn't worth the effort. The collective is nearly ready to shut down the experiments. Our ships need to be better amplifiers."

"Why do we feel gravitational down direction on the ship?" Ted tapped his foot on the deck. "We maintain a base one void below us all; just enough to simulate gravity and each of us has a weak offsetting void to counter the ship's field. Because you and Liz are here, it mimics 9.8 meters per second, per second like the Earth's surface. For my species, it could be different, but this is fine. Part of our acclimatization to Earth duty is to become used to an Earth one g force.

"Creating that artificial gravity also affects our course and is another reason we use an arced trajectory. It's as if we have made ourselves into a ballistic object. The ship wants to fall up in that artificial gravity we feel."

"In our science fiction, they invented inertial stabilizers to explain ship-board gravity. It made making movies easier." Siglinde said.

"You could call what we do inertial field generation." Ted said. "We are all little Star Trek space ships."

"I don't feel like a spaceship." Siglinde said.

"You don't look like one either." Ted said.

He leaned over; their lips met.

"Get a room," Liz walked in, accompanied by an alien in their shimmering grey. Liz saw an easy familiarity between the pair and she wondered if Liz had found a new lover. Liz had had to give up her last one to get security clearance to join Siglinde's alien hunters. Apparently, lesbian socialist geologists were not on the NSA's approved list.

"I could fix you up if you're jealous," Ted smiled.

The alien with Liz suddenly transformed into a voluptuous, scantily clad Earth woman who seemed to be from a Las Vegas show. The apparition batted her eyes at Liz.

"Don't toy with me. Maybe I'll get a better offer on the planet, maybe someone with brains."

"Maybe you could have both." The seductress winked and reverted to their shimmering grey form whose gender only another alien could discern.

"Where did you find that form?" Ted asked his alien crewmate.

"RoH," she replied in English. "She saw that woman on a poster hanging in a Nevada gas station."

"Say no more," Ted laughed. "You've been hanging around Earth too long, and the RoH Show goes everywhere. Who knew Ellie's daughter could teach star travellers humour and humans humility all at the same time?"

Liz Davis stared at her alien friend, then at Ted and Siglinde.

Is Siglinde just living some bizarre fantasy with Ted, an imposter human? She thought. *Will he hurt her?*

"No, Liz," Ted said aloud, "and stop being the anthropologist. This is supposed to be a vacation for you."

Actually, Ted could not say why he had invited Liz on this honeymoon trip with his partner, Siglinde. RoH's father had sent the idea, and Ted had not questioned it. Perhaps the alien community had a reason. Since RoH had affected them with human spontaneous curiosity, perhaps it was just a whim. Still, the alien mind did nothing without purpose. Then he looked at Siglinde.

I did not fall in love on purpose, Ted thought.

"Damn, I wish I could do that... read minds, I mean," Liz said.

"We'll explore to see if perhaps some gene splicing might let you." Liz's alien companion said and touched her hand.

"Me too... me too," Siglinde said and kissed Ted on the lips.

"It seems you already can," Ted returned the kiss, then turned away and said, "Liz, the anthropologist and Siglinde, the quantum physicist, will find a lot to interest them on our honeymoon moon."

"This star-bus of yours has already interested me." Siglinde said. "The control room, or whatever you call it, blew my mind. I half-expected to find a star ship bridge from a movie or five catatonic zombies in the seats. The operators seem relaxed, and it threw me off. I saw no blinking lights or heard a sound."

"I've been in one of those seats often, but not on this trip. Once we are in deep space, there is less to do. Maintaining the quantum void does not demand much concentration unless we travel near gravity wells. That's why we arc above the galactic plane where the primary field is the galaxy focused on its central mass. Even though space between Earth and Z263-A is relatively empty, out here, there are fewer random dead bodies and less dust for us to deal with, and that makes it easier."

"That massive black hole," Siglinde smiled.

"It is the centre for sure, but we sum all the fields with it, and nearby stars have more influence on the ship. We use several galaxies in the local group to track our position, like Earth's ocean navigators used Polaris, or your spacecraft use stars to navigate in your solar system. We will travel only seven of Earth parsecs on this trip, but a small deviation would make for a big miss in the end. The operators are mostly tweaking now."

"Only seven," Siglinde said. "How far have we travelled? We left Earth two days ago."

"We are doing about two parsecs each Earth day, so we are not yet halfway to Z263-A. The arcing course adds to the distance."

Siglinde thought about that final, chaotic day at home. She had made frantic calls to her family, telling them she would be on a secret government assignment for a few months, and yes, it had to do with the aliens, and no, she would be safe and in excellent hands. Siglinde had not found the way to tell her mother that good alien arms would also hold her. She did mention she had a special friend named Ted.

"When are you getting married?" Mom asked.

"Now love," Siglinde heard her father's voice offscreen in the video call. "Don't push the girl. She's in love with electrons and you just want some grand baby quantum quarks to cuddle."

Her father had come into view.

"Look, baby, just make sure. And if you're serious, make the bond covalent, not some namby-pamby ionic thing that could lead to repulsion."

He had laughed. Her father taught science in a high school and his lame dad jokes held a little sophistication. Mother had trained as a horticulturist and ran a garden centre. She loved to nurture and always hoped for little ones to play with among the hostas.

"I might turn up and surprise you." Siglinde could not tell her family directly that she would have an alien double on Earth who might make it seem Siglinde had not disappeared. Siglinde did not know that her Earthly doppelgänger would assume a high-profile public role.

Liz told no one, relying on her duplicate to seem like the real Liz. Her sexuality had estranged her from her family.

Ted, of course, had no earthly connections to massage.

Siglinde did not feel as if they had fled Earth, but she did not know why the aliens might want her and Liz off the planet. Her safety, and that she and Ted were taking a honeymoon, seemed the obvious reasons. He had simply given Liz a reward because he liked her. It had been the residents of Z263-A that had specifically requested the two women, and the aliens did not know why.

The National Agency for Aerial Phenomena still functioned as an American government agency with their alien surrogates filling in. The President, attempting to benefit from the alien arrival, would not know that three NAAP leaders were alien doppelgänger stand-ins.

"Siglinde," Ted took her hand, "you have already learned some of our science that is decades, if not a century, ahead of where Earth's knowledge should be. You will learn much more. If the rest of humanity makes the right choices now, then you can return and lead the science that will resolve many problems, at least the Earth's energy problem. If they do not, your knowledge loose on the planet would hasten destruction and put you in danger. In that case, you and Liz will remain here or return to a dying Earth where everyone would think you were crackpots. Ellie and RoH work hard to prevent that, but the uncertainty is huge. I, for one, never want to hear RoH cry, and for sure, I don't want to lose you."

Ted tenderly kissed Siglinde.

"I know you both will miss Earth," the other alien said, "but hopefully, we will return soon. You will find Jewel relaxing and interesting. The locals eagerly expect your arrival, and even more so, seeing more of what Ellie Keys calls the 'RoH Show.' The antics of Ellie's daughter on Earth have excited the locals on Jewel. It thrills us too, but we hope to find out why Jewel has such an interest in RoH. Perhaps you will help us understand the place better. There is something about Jewel that eludes us."

"We think the residents of Z263-A deliberately prevented us from knowing," Ted said. "They shield their minds from us and have only permitted us to have brief visits to a small part of the planet. They seem more eager to have humans visit."

Ted thought he knew the answer to Siglinde's question of why he had brought her on the trip. Ted's species needed an excuse to send a representative to Jewel, to send Ted hopefully to unlock Jewel's secret. Even though Siglinde was the only entity in the galaxy that he loved, Ted could not tell her these details. He knew the people of Jewel could read her mind, and he telling his lover why the trip happened lay in the hands of the collective approval. He could not decide on his own.

Ted did not know, because the lien collective had no suspicion, that another layer of interest drove these events. Z263-A was the nexus of a new galactic arrangement beyond the wildest speculation of human and alien. The Andromeda issue drove necessity.

"I hope I discover more," Liz donned her anthropologist hat. "Damn it, I find you all an exciting mystery."

"My species is much like you, Liz," Ted said. "We first visited Earth as anthropologists, curious and excited to watch human development. It soon experienced the darkness of recent human history. The development of the atomic bomb in 1945 disappointed us. We saw it, rightly, as too much power, too soon for humans to control. We had no hope for your success until 1947. Lust and love in Lubbock, Texas changed everything. That gave us Ellie, and now her daughter, RoH. We want to understand Jewel as well, but the inhabitants have such mental power that we cannot, unless they will share the information. Jewel is still a mystery, and we don't like to find a mental power greater than ours."

CHAPTER 2

Planet fall

Brilliant as a blob of quicksilver, it shone on the chalk-grey oblate of the planet's moon: a jewel amid a ruin of decay.
- John Brunner

Many describe the galaxy as a cosmic pinball machine. Others see it as elegant clockwork. Perhaps both are right. In a universe of frequent collisions, explosions and chaos, majestic spheres revolve and rotate in a precise dance. Stars orbit galaxies, planets orbit stars and moons orbit planets. In this developed beauty, there remains room for habitable moons to orbit impossibly huge planets that revolve around stable, life-giving suns. Such a system is Z263-A.

Earth knew the nurturing star as Sigma Draconis, or Alsafi, to the ancient Arabs and Tin Chú in even older Chinese knowledge. The complex alien coordinate and descriptive designation did not matter, and for human simplicity they had reduced it to Z263-A, meaning the habitable moon itself, Jewel in local lore.

The ship arched above the massive central planet and its Earth-size moon; Jewel rose beyond the horizon, a jewel shining in the star's beauty. The humans watched in real time from their usual forward view port. Siglinde felt no acceleration as they descended towards a sphere that, strangely, looked like Earth. The blue of its vast seas soon held swaths of cloud, and solid land appeared in brown, yellow, and green detail. An island near one continent shone like a cluster of diamonds and reflected the bright sun.

To Siglinde, the star, Sigma Draconis seemed slightly more yellow than Sol, but she guessed the view port might cause that. Her mental questions raised a spontaneous display on the port showing the physical characteristics of Sigma D, the mass, surface temperature and other basic measurements in Earth units as the ship reacted to her thoughts. The display emphasized the fact that the entire alien community functioned as vast organic intelligence, with its individuals as complexly inter-connected as the human brain, and that included artefacts like spaceships.

The same fundamental information for Z263-A followed, and it almost duplicated Earth: gravity, atmosphere and all. Its period of rotation showed as 25 hours. The precision startled Siglinde.

Did someone create Z263-A as a clone of Earth, similar to my doppelgänger back in Washington? The energy needed would be fantastic.

The idea seemed preposterous to Siglinde.

"We think it's natural," Ted said.

Siglinde, in love, had encouraged Ted to share her mind. She wished she could do the same with him.

"Even with our abilities," Ted said, "we could not create Jewel from scratch. The locals have not allowed us to explore and determine Jewel's geologic history."

"If not your people, then who?" Siglinde asked

"Nobody," Ted said. "It would be impossible and has to be a natural coincidence."

Siglinde did not like coincidences. In all the exotic planets human astronomers had found, only a few came close to Earth and none matched it so well.

"We," Ted said, meaning his star family, "don't like coincidences either. It upsets us that there seem to be two options; it's an artefact or the result of natural processes. We have searched for other bodies of this physical type in our records and in our explorations. This is the only one so far."

Ted frowned.

The ship levelled into a low orbit around Jewel. Water covered most of the moon with several large, Australia size islands and one massive continent.

Several smaller islands sparkled in the sun and Siglinde thought they might occupy geodetic points. Their course brought them towards the dominant land mass.

"Why isn't Jewel tidal-locked with the big planet?" Siglinde asked.

"It's far from the planet and the process hasn't developed to make it always face the parent." Ted said, "It suggests a young age, but we don't know its original rotation or its geologic past."

Ted mentally shared the complete story of the history between the star travellers and Jewel. Ted's species had first reached Jewel about a thousand Earth years before. The aliens had not seen the moon in earlier surveys, and thought that the inhabitants of Jewel had deliberately screened themselves, but mysteriously appeared in the past millennium. Its inhabitants had equal, perhaps greater, quantum abilities to the star species and could have reached the stars, but they had remained on their home moon. Liz wanted to find out why.

Unlike what they had done on Earth with its more primitive development, Ted's species could not research the anthropology and history of Jewel. They only knew what the locals told them. While not arrogant, the aliens had always had unhindered access to everything in the galaxy. Jewel gave them a lesson in humility.

The craft dropped into the atmosphere above the super-continent with no effect until they shot through a high cloud layer. Then, Siglinde felt vertigo at the impossible speed of their descent to a spot some distant from the coastline. In an instant they hovered a few meters above a flat plain, a grass covered meadow complete with a variety of flowers dancing in the breeze. The calming effect of the dancing blooms mesmerized the human.

An alien crewmember floated their luggage towards them as the view port became a doorway. Ted took Siglinde's hand; they stepped into a warm breeze and eased down the few metres, seemingly on an invisible elevator, to the colourful field. Liz and the baggage followed. The meadow appeared to be empty.

"What, no hula girls?" Liz asked.

"You would love them, but I wouldn't," Siglinde grabbed Ted's hand, "they might steal this guy."

In the distance, a lone, bipedal figure approached, solid and sure among the waving flowers. It stood two meters high, neither human nor alien, silver, with a spherical sensor-covered head, manipulator arms, and smoothly functioning legs.

The machine, Siglinde, thought of it as a machine, stopped in front of Ted and waited. Siglinde felt a brief flash of uncertainty and briefly wondered if she needed her mother's arms for safety like when she had been little and afraid. The Earthlings could not sense the exchange between Ted and the otherworldly entity.

The robot touched Ted and said, "Species 2."

It touched Siglinde and Liz, and its head jerked up. "Species preliminary assignment is Nova-1, human, and a pure version of the Ellie/Species 2 sub-variant."

Ted laughed. "Hey Robbie, wait until you meet RoH."

"I have met both her and her organic mother. Why do you call me Robbie?" the greeter asked.

Ted touched the machine and transferred the Earth movie Forbidden Planet into its brain.

"Don't call me Robbie." The robot said with a sound that Siglinde understood as laughter. This machine had a sense of humour. The brief mental exchange told Ted the machine had cultural depth, but he waited for it to reveal itself.

"Our honeymoon will be a barrel of laughs, Honey." Siglinde said.

"Smart for a gal who just made her first quantum leap," Ted laughed.

"Stop with the movie jokes." Liz said.

"I love Earth's rustic culture." Ted hugged Siglinde. Over her shoulder, he saw Liz taking notes. She noticed.

"You are a very interesting specimen, Ted Kotwas of Species 2," Liz winked.

"So are you, pure variant of Nova-1, Human."

"Welcome..." the greeter said to the women in smooth English and then paused. What might have been optical sensors focused on Ted, then on Siglinde and suddenly changed into a likeness of...

"Mother..." Siglinde shrieked, "Ted..." her horrified look speared into her lover.

Ted waved at the apparition and suddenly Ted's high school math teacher, a middle-aged female human, appeared in place of the miscalculation. Ted hugged Siglinde to calm her trembles.

"I'm sorry I upset you. I acted on imperfect knowledge," the math teacher said. "Please forgive me Ms. Hilfreich. I'll be careful now."

Siglinde shuddered, speechless.

"What are you?" Liz ignored her friend's upset. "I saw a robot, and now you look human."

"I'm neither of those," the teacher said. "We thought the robot might be more familiar to human cultural expectations for an alien world."

"Forbidden Planet," Ted smirked.

The math teacher scowled at Ted as if he had fumbled a differential.

"As you saw, we can make mistakes." "I owe you the courtesy of being myself. Here I am."

A figure replaced the teacher, much shorter with long dark hair, a burnished copper face and apparently human, dressed in a loose tan smock.

Female, Liz thought, *and beautiful.*

"Yes, in a binary species, in Earth terms, I am a female named Anya; however, we have fluid gender and there are unlimited variations, many spirits some call it. I understand, on Earth there is sometimes violent disagreement over gender and its dynamic reality. If that ever existed here, it lies beyond any of our remembered history. I appreciate your judgement of my appearance. It is what Mater always says."

"How do you reproduce?" Liz assumed these people would share the indifference to personal questions that her star travelling friends had. For the moment, she would ignore who Mater might be.

"We don't birth often, but you name it," Anya said, "everything from orgasmic intercourse to in vitro. Everyone likes to have fun and physical interactions can have the variety of our gender choices and whatever pleasure is acceptable. We control reproduction and few encounters result in a newborn."

Anya's gaze fell on Liz. Liz's cheeks warmed.

"I will explore this later. Take me to your leader." Liz laughed.

"We are the leader," Anya said.

"We...?" Liz could see no one besides Anya. She glanced at Ted and Siglinde for help.

"Now that we are here," Ted said, "they have made us part of them, the population, and so that makes us part of the leader, part of the 'we' of this entire sentient population. Our community lives as an extended entity with mental connection," Ted said, "an organism, if you will. The population of Jewel is more so. Like Earth's tribal people, but mentally linked, although we can only take part verbally. Even though we are outsiders, our thoughts contribute to the sum of things to be considered."

Ted frowned at Anya, who nodded.

"So you see," she said. "It includes all life here. I am to familiarize you with Jewel and will guide you. I am honoured. Interesting aliens are a treat. Where would you go?"

Ted stood passively, but Liz and Siglinde's faces reflected confused uncertainty. They knew nothing of Jewel and remained at Anya's mercy.

Anya read a thought of a house and a bed from Siglinde. She immediately understood that the human required a stable home base to feel comfortable.

"Ah, of course, shelters, unnecessary here, but please, follow me."

Anya led them towards where the dancing flowers merged with the blue sky. Their baggage dutifully floated behind them. Distance had somehow compressed, and they soon reached a sharp boundary between the meadow and a mixed forest. Anya waved her hand, and they walked into the trees. When Siglinde looked back, she saw that a barren, dusty plain had replaced the meadow beyond the sharp edge of the forest. Their ship had disappeared into the blue sky but remained in stationary orbit high above.

"What happened to the land?" Siglinde asked.

"We prepared the meadow in welcome," Anya said, "so that you would feel our happiness at your coming. We have expected you since you left Earth, even before that. Visitors are so infrequent, and we have been told that humans are interesting."

"We find them interesting," Ted said and squeezed Siglinde's hand.

"If we did not know, or perhaps did not like whoever arrived, it might have been a sterile, paved landing zone." Anya said. "It would be likely we would never allow such a visitor to land. Few others visit us. We isolate ship arrivals, the equivalent of an air lock in space, protection against contamination. Your vessel passed examination, but we keep the welcoming place isolated."

"A force field," Siglinde said.

"More or less," Anya replied. "Otherwise, most of our planet is in a natural state, and we are in that normal part now. Everything you see is as the planet, in its wisdom, has decided. We are humble and do not interfere."

There is something not right here, Liz thought.

Anya touched her hand and said,

"Everything is as we know it should be. Jewel is Jewel and is what you see."

The poetic line calmed but did not convince the questioning scientist. Anya noticed. Liz would be her project. She liked the thought.

CHAPTER 3

Art

"teaching him, as best she can, the business of living."
— *Ted Chiang, The Lifecycle of Software Objects*

The accommodations appeared through the trees and resembled Earth holiday cottages.

"We made one for you as a binary couple, and my friend Liz will have the other. I trust this satisfies you." Anya said. "Liz, come with me, and I'll show you your Jewel home."

Anya took Liz's hand and drew her deeper into the forest.

As Anya and Liz went beyond to the second dwelling, Ted and Siglinde turned to an Earth-like squared-stone house. The smoky quartz blocks met closely, and no mortar joined them. The structure seemed to be new, but showed no signs of construction. Forest began only a few metres away and surrounded the building. The large coniferous trees resembled Earth's red pines. The ground beneath lay open with no large undergrowth and dead needles covered the ground in a soft carpet. A forest biologist would have noted the maturity of the litter and that it had no sign of ever suffering a forest fire. The forest resembled a garden.

Ted and Siglinde entered, and light from an invisible source filled the interior. A large living area greeted them with no vestibule from the door.

"There's no place for boots, coats and hats," Siglinde said.

"I don't think they have seasons here," Ted said. "They have no need of outerwear. It sure isn't upstate New York."

"It's bright," Siglinde said.

The lighting dimmed to a comfortable level.

A large rug overlay the centre of a hardwood floor. The wood grain resembled quarter cut oak that ran in long strips about 12 centimetres wide. They had painted the walls a flat mist green that offered relaxation. A stuffed couch with leather upholstery took one wall with a matching recliner chair sitting askew to one side. A hand-hooked wall-hanging that spread above the couch depicted a beach, aqua-green waters and shining mountains on the horizon. The place matched the familiar layout of her condominium home in Virginia right down to the wall hanging, except hers depicted a quiet country lane and a homey white cottage. In a difference to Siglinde's Virginia condominium, there were no extra lamps and no television. Other than feeling like a psychiatrist's waiting room, it offered the same comfort as Siglinde's Earth home.

It's sure familiar. Perhaps they got the layout from my head, like Anya imitating Mother, Siglinde thought. *I'm glad I didn't think of that undergrad dorm room I shared with Jasmine.*

"The kitchen is through that doorway," Siglinde nodded. She led Ted into a bright, sterile room with a large table and chair set and with the usual North American clutter of counter top appliances and the standard large ones.

Siglinde opened a refrigerator and discovered her favourite foods.

"Did you send a menu ahead?" She asked.

"No," Ted laughed and leaned against an Earth-like kitchen stove. I guess Anya read your mind."

"That's what I think," Siglinde said, "but how could they have filled these cupboards so quickly?"

Siglinde saw fixtures identical to what she had had on Earth. She opened several drawers, and all were empty except for the cutlery drawer, where it should be near the stove. The lower cupboards had pots and pans, baking pans, and cookie sheets. Siglinde had had these in Virginia, but she mostly used the coffee-maker and the microwave oven.

Thousands of places in North America look just like this; she thought to explain its similarity to her condominium. The kitchen floor startled her. It exactly duplicated the staggered cream and grey tiles she had had specially installed to mimic the familiarity of her mother's kitchen. When she was a little girl, she and Mom, and later her friends, played hop-scotch on the kitchen floor. Siglinde smiled at the warm memory.

Siglinde poured a glass of cold juice that looked like pink lemonade, but it had orange-juice flavour. The container showed a picture of a strange fruit. She retrieved a cookie that tasted like oatmeal from the small pantry cupboard where it should have been and washed it down with the juice.

"If I didn't feel so comfortable, and knowing I'm safe with you, this place might creep me out."

Siglinde hugged Ted.

"I know it looks a lot like your place," Ted said, "but Anya's little shape-shifting gave us a clue about how this place might work. I don't think you need to be afraid, but I would sure like to understand."

Ted did not feel fear for himself. Aliens never feared, even in the face of death.

"I don't know what we will eat," Siglinde said. "All I see here is juice and snacks, even if all the cooking paraphernalia is here. I can't see anything for breakfast."

Siglinde revisited the refrigerator and discovered eggs and bacon that she had not noticed the first time. A sudden feeling of disconnect hit Siglinde. She swept her eyes around the room as if something might lurk there.

"I need some fresh air," she said. "I'll miss seeing the sky. Trees surround the place and are gorgeous, but I love a vista. It looked like we were embedded in the forest."

She led Ted through the back door.

The back yard startled Siglinde. Instead of the deep forest she had expected, it comprised a natural meadow with pleasing shrubbery and flowers in a natural jumble.

The field gently sloped away and exposed a vast swath of sky. From the sun angle, Siglinde guessed they looked north.

"I think you're right, Love, that's north, in Earth's system." Ted hugged her and drew her to a bench. "We landed near the terminator and night is falling. This system has spectacular star patterns, and because of the parent planet's magnetic field, remarkable auroras."

"Jewel now orbits on the side of the mother planet away from the star, so tonight will be dark. The major planet will be a disk in the sky most of the day. Ted pointed to the arc of the mother planet as it neared the western horizon. Morning or evening twilight can linger longer as we pass to the star side, and when the planet is in our night sky, we won't have deep darkness because of planet shine. As a matter of fact, it will be damned bright. It's a good thing there aren't lunatics on Jewel." Ted laughed. "Jewel is just far enough away, and its orbit inclined slightly so that it never enters the shadow of the mother planet. There are no eclipses. We understand the orbits and anything we can examine from afar, but we know little about the residents of the planet."

"It seems almost deliberate," Siglinde said. "I swear this looked like a forest when we arrived."

"I think you are right. It was all forest. I have never travelled this far on Jewel before," Ted said. "It's as if our surroundings respond to our thoughts, but it keeps us ignorant. We must consider this."

Ted sent his question to the ship above and it would spread through the local diaspora of Species 2. He also puzzled over why they numbered his species as 2.

Who is species one? I assume they mean the people of Jewel.

Perhaps the fleet would have some answers, but he did not think it would be soon. That the answer would come through the importance of RoH, the hybrid girl would not be a surprise, but on earth she still pursued the renegade human/alien hybrid and the time for truth had not yet arrived.

It would take some time before they could understand the reality of Jewel, and it would not come from Ted's community, but from Species 1.

This is too perfect. Siglinde frowned. She snuggled against Ted, sighed and thought of gentle nights on an Earthly hillside.

"I love to hear the forest sounds at night. So far, I haven't even heard a bird chirp."

As the sky darkened, birds squawked and settled for the night. The chirp of crickets softened the dusk and a distant owl hooted. Siglinde thought it imitated the increasing sound that opened many movies. She imagined a being at a sound board raising the volume of nature's creatures.

Why am I hearing birds now? Siglinde thought. *It is so peaceful, but it feels contrived.*

In the gentleness of the twilight, Siglinde felt all of her cares; thoughts and even her hopes wash away. As the stars filled the sky, she sensed an oneness with it all: the forest, the sky, Ted, life, as if the planet and the cosmos had embraced her. She remembered as a little girl, perhaps five years old, enfolded in her parents' arms, washed by a Vermont sunset.

The sky blazed with stars, but in unfamiliar patterns from earthly imagination.

"This place needs some old shepherds to name the constellations," Siglinde said. "I think one looks like a dog."

Siglinde pointed.

"You're nuts," Ted said.

Siglinde and Ted cuddled on the bench, lost in the beauty, until sleep called them inside.

Siglinde's questions about meals received an answer at breakfast time.

A robot that resembled a mechanical Jeeves the butler had arrived and prepared breakfast after Siglinde and Ted awakened. While bi-pedal, the device could not be mistaken for human, or indeed, organic.

The visitors sat at the kitchen table, and the thing carried two steaming cups of coffee in mechanical hands that resembled miniature ice-hockey gloves that could flow around and grip any object it wished to hold. Its optical sensors focused on its guests as it placed the cups onto the table. The machine had remarkable dexterity.

"Have a seat," Siglinde took a small sip and waved the bi-pedal machine to a chair as if it were a human friend over for a visit.

"The force vectors that apply to my mobility device are at their optimum if I stand at stasis." It said. The soft voice sounded human, with an English purity that hid any accent.

Californian or Canadian, Siglinde thought, and focused on the hockey hands.

The machine placed two plates of food onto the table, stood feet slightly apart, hung its simulated arms loosely, and awaited orders.

"Mobility device...?" Siglinde asked.

"What you call your body," the machine replied, as if separating its mechanical side from its thinking ability.

"Sophisticated species have developed a language of the essential," Ted said. "The human body, in fact all organic bodies," Ted tapped his chest, "incorporate a fascinating number of various components, but they all work to support mobility and manipulation and those find nourishment for the total body. A robot has simple systems to perform those functions. Unlike our living bodies, mobility is unnecessary to find its food to support the other essential components, so it can focus on other tasks. It only eats energy and spare parts. Robbie has reduced his self-image to the mechanical."

"I am designated, AR64-T. I am unfamiliar with Robbie."

"Okay," Ted said, "We'll call you ART."

"Hello, Art, it's nice to meet you." Siglinde extended a hand.

"Art...," the machine pondered its new designation and entered it into his response protocols. Art touched her middle finger with its equivalent and Siglinde felt as if her fingertip had slid into warm jelly. She at first felt spooked, but then filled with reassurance, as if Art sent comfort through the touch.

"Eat," Art said. "I will open your anti-photon shields."

Art rolled up the heavy window blinds.

"Art," Siglinde said, "I don't even think RoH could teach you poetry or make you smile."

"RoH visited some time ago, but did not teach. She learned. She did not have that name then, and I did not meet her. RoH is of special importance."

"Maybe I can get you to lighten up." Siglinde said.

Art developed a strong glow.

"Is this okay, Siglinde?"

Siglinde sighed and then laughed.

"Go back to the way you were. I wouldn't want you breathing hard."

Art reverted to his normal state.

"I don't breath."

"I don't think you'll ever be a poet, but maybe we can teach you some Earth English idioms. Ted, can we get Steve Jorgensen here to help Art?"

"Steve might be here anyway, with Ellie, if things don't go well on Earth. We should have an update soon."

Steve Jorgensen was a linguist, and partner of Ellie Keys, RoH's mother. The necessity that forced Siglinde and Liz to take a vacation on Jewel might force all aliens working on Earth and their human friends to flee. Convincing humans to do better occupied Ellie's efforts. A dangerous rogue human-alien hybrid had distracted her daughter, RoH.

Ellie linked humans to the star travellers. She had been the ultimate experiment in interbreeding on Earth. Ellie's existence had introduced compassion, love, and empathy into the alien culture. Her daughter, RoH, seemed to be the perhaps last development in that effort. She awed both humans and star travellers and had mysteriously attracted the interest of Jewel's natives.

Was RoH interesting enough on her one visit here? There is something about RoH I don't understand. Siglinde thought.

Siglinde considered these things. She could never guess at the reality of the being called RoH, or of the planet called Jewel. Art focused on her and waved his arms in some form of machine emotion.

"RoH, as you call her, is special," Art said. "RoH is..." Art's arms waved again, and he seemed at a loss for words.

"Of unknown importance," Ted finished Art's sentence.

"She talked to Jewel, you know. RoH and Jewel have a bond. We don't understand."

"You mean the people of Jewel, of course. How can someone talk to a planet?" Siglinde asked.

"No, Jewel, the planet, but we don't understand," Art repeated. "RoH might return."

Siglinde thought the machine, the sentient artefact they called Art, sounded defeated, as if no knowledge should escape the denizens of Jewel. Perhaps the sentient beings here did not even understand their planet. In this, they had something in common with Siglinde and Ted's Species 2, and she was partly right in thinking that the people of

Jewel considered themselves as Species 1. Siglinde led in another direction.

"Can you change shapes, imitate other beings?" Siglinde asked.

"No," Art said, "service devices are mechanical. It would not be helpful but confusing to appear as an organic being on Jewel. We would not be doing a physical transformation, but a mental cloak imposed on people around us. We do not have that ability and not designed for that, and even so would require too much energy for an artefact such as me."

"But they can appear to be like you." Siglinde smiled.

"As you saw yesterday, the organics can appear to you as they wish, even look like me, with little effort or energy needed, but the mechanical that Anya mimicked yesterday did not, as you see, resemble me, and it was only in your perception. Anya was physically there. Apparently, they follow a rule never to imitate us. They only do it for visitors. No organic changes on Jewel otherwise."

Siglinde remembered RoH showing her quantum mental trickery when they had first met. RoH had provided the same information that Art now shared. Ellie had once said that her daughter, RoH, could change her appearance easily, as if she changed socks.

Siglinde looked at her lover, Ted, who appeared all too human to her. He felt human as well, but she knew he had to spend his entire time tricking her brain. It must have taken a lot of his energy and thinking power to do it. She took his hand for reassurance.

Perhaps it reflects his love for me. She thought.

"Siglinde," Ted said, "I manipulate my appearance, but not your perception. My Earth form is as real as you, even if it requires effort. And yes, I love you."

Ted hugged Liz, and she felt his warmth. He felt human.

"Art, do all of you mechanicals look alike?" Siglinde asked.

"There is no need for other biped designs," Art said, "But there are those with specific functions, food provision and so on. Some of these cannot move; some move on wheels, tracks or over two legs. Sometimes a work unit must rise above the surface. When that happens, an organic, a person, as you would say, works with the robot and raises it to the work using quantum gravity manipulation. Machines do not have that ability. I am a multi-functional entity of general purpose and can perform most tasks, although not as efficiently as a specific."

"How will we know it is you with us?"

"I am the only mechanical to help you. They assigned one to your friend Liz, but that will stay at her abode as I will here. Anya has elected to escort Liz. The organics like to interact with each other, the personal touch, as you humans say."

Siglinde was not sure if Art had expressed a robotic chuckle, an organic trait that might mean he found the animal species amusing. It also might mean it... he... could think and perhaps have a personality beyond his mentioned programming. It might be self-aware.

"I find organic traits curious," Art said. "Siglinde, as you see, I heard your thoughts, but if you wish, I will no longer do so. It helps me care for you more efficiently."

"It sounds like they have you robots on a short leash." Siglinde said.

Art seemed confused, but then gave a sound that Siglinde once again considered a chuckle.

"You confused me," Art said. "We don't have dogs on Jewel. I had never heard the word leash before."

"You should have dogs here," Siglinde said. "You might have fun."

Art paused, but then became businesslike.

"I will care for you, but soon you will meet other Oshki and they will be with you. I will remain here; ready to help when you are near."

"For now, I would appreciate it if you didn't look in my head," Siglinde said. "If you think I am in danger, then you may do it, or when I tell you."

"You will never be in danger on Jewel," Art and Ted said together. Ted laughed, but Art remained passive.

"What if I fall out of a tree or off a cliff...?" Siglinde said. She seemed to be serious.

"Organics never climb trees or hang over cliffs." Art said.

"You have never met a Nova Species, Human." Siglinde laughed.

"She has you there, Art. Siglinde might not behave." Ted said.

"If you do something dangerous, your organic guide will keep you safe," Art said.

"Will we meet many organics?" Siglinde asked. "Please don't keep saying organic units. Can you find another word for the people of Jewel?"

"Jewelians," Ted laughed.

"Try simply, people," Siglinde glared at Ted.

Art ignored the lovers' teasing.

"The organic inhabitants of Jewel, at least these call themselves Oshki," Art said. "There are others, far beyond the waters, beyond the Crystal Mountains. They do not interact. Their interaction with Jewel differs from the Oshki."

"So, Anya is Oshki?"

"Yes..."

"You will not meet many Oshki," "They have a dispersed population that reduces disease threats. Even with suitable treatment methods, prevention is better than a cure."

"That's why they isolate visitors until they are sure." Ted said.

"Exactly," Art said, "the population lives in small groups over the parts of Jewel that have a gentle climate. Some choose to live in hard places, but these still suffer no discomfort. Jewel has no seasons as Earth has, so the polar areas are only lightly ice covered. They have cooler weather from time to time and have no inhabitants. The Oshki can control local conditions."

"It sounds like paradise," Siglinde said, "but maybe too isolated and too good to be true. In an Earth movie, the planet would turn into a dangerous, sentient monster."

"Not dangerous, not a monster," Art said. "Oshki have achieved an ideal stasis, and isolation is not a problem. They can mentally communicate anywhere on the surface and beyond. As for Jewel being sentient, ask RoH about that."

"Beyond the planet, how do they do that?" Siglinde asked. "Who are the others beyond the sea?"

Art waved his mechanical arms as if agitated.

"I have said too much. It is not for me to explain." Art fell silent, but seemed concerned, as if he had divulged a secret.

Siglinde thought Art was a more complex entity than a mere mechanical. She saw him as self-aware and able to learn, but not creative from within. That certainly differentiated him from humans, and Siglinde wondered if it also distinguished him from the Oshki. She only had Anya as an example of Oshki, and Siglinde understood Anya had all the human traits and much more. She eagerly waited to meet more Oshki.

"Will Anya arrive soon?" Ted sensed the machine's confusion and opened another path.

"She will stay with Liz. She likes that human. Another will arrive shortly to be your mentor."

Art cleared the table and began mundane household chores that Ted thought might be busy work to avoid more questions. Ted led Siglinde outside into the morning shade of the forest.

"I am upset," Ted said. "Art acted as if he had said too much, but I can't penetrate his mental shield. I should be able easily to sense any quantum process. Anya was more open, but I could only touch her mind when she allowed it. Art seems to decide on what to say. I think it is more than a programmed machine."

"Why would they need to be dispersed to prevent sickness? I thought your species controlled infections using quantum intervention." Siglinde said.

"We do," Ted said. "I think they have low densities for another reason. Perhaps there are fewer Oshki than Art suggested. My family maintains low densities on planets to prevent stressing our habitat, which is this bit of the galaxy."

"You never told me how many of your species live in the galaxy." Siglinde said. "Even around Earth, the thousands of you are far outnumbered by humans. Of course, you out-gun us."

"Humans need to stop thinking in terms of guns," Ted said. "Our technology is superior, but we have no guns."

"You know what I mean," Siglinde said.

Ted fell silent. He knew Siglinde's heart and simply hoped that RoH and Ellie could help humanity change to that level of understanding and love. He also knew that star traveller's quantum abilities far exceeded the power of any Earth weapon. Unlike humans with the fusion bomb, aliens were mature enough to never use quantum manipulation as a weapon.

Ted hugged his lover. She almost understood that quantum mental power was the key to it all. Once she made that breakthrough, Ted knew he had to help Siglinde keep the secret until humans had decided on peace.

"I feel peaceful," Siglinde snuggled against Ted and hoped to cheer him, "but I can't hear one bird this morning. That's strange, as if the place only has night birds."

Faint chirping similar to Earth sparrows began, accompanied by the caw of a crow."

Siglinde frowned.

That's convenient, she thought. *As if the forest read my mind. The same thing happened last night.*

"Hello," the voice startled them. Neither Siglinde nor Ted had heard the approach, but the needle covered forest floor hid all footsteps. An old man dressed as a woodsman drew near.

Chapter 4

Liz and Anya

After climbing a great hill, one only finds that there are many more hills to climb.
- Nelson Mandela

"Good morning, Liz." Anya entered Liz's dwelling in the woods, unannounced. The residents of Jewel did not consider personal space.

"I'm sorry if I have offended you," Anya felt Liz's discomfort, but also Liz's sudden brightening at her arrival. Anya smiled. Being with this human gave feelings of pleasure that none of her Oshki brothers or sister had ever provided. Maybe it was the alien's dark skinned beauty, but perhaps more the visitor's lively mind. Anya hoped Liz would learn to enjoy her company as much as she now relished hers.

"I am so sorry, Liz. I did not mean to surprise you."

Anya hoped she had not harmed their relationship.

"We do not guard secrets on Jewel and feel no embarrassment or guilt. Our intentions are obvious and never harmful. I had eagerness to be with you. I hope we bond and have no secrets."

Liz blushed, although her dark skin hid it. Anya had flattered her, and that uncommon feeling surprised the down-to-earth scientist. Anya's burnished, copper-coloured face remained un-readable.

"Maybe, when I get to know you better, I'll want you to read my mind. I must learn to fit in," Liz repeated the mantra from her anthropological field research. She tried to shift her distracted mind to field-research mode.

"I am your guest here."

"Once you are here, you are part of us," Anya referred to the definition of "we" that Ted had explained yesterday.

"I don't feel that," Liz said.

"Maybe I can help you overcome Earth based conventions and show you our way. We are totally open about everything."

Anya eyed Liz, searching for a reaction. Even though she could probe, she would not enter her new friend's mind without Liz allowing it. She followed another rule that her people held dear when building a relationship. Anya desperately wanted to avoid angering or frightening Liz.

"This is new." Liz said. "Even in the most open and loving tribal villages I visited, they maintained some private, personal space. I would love learning from you,"

Liz felt comfortable with this alien.

No, not an alien, a woman, a resident of Jewel who could be my friend, Liz thought. *I have much to learn and gain here.*

Being a scientist, Liz had struggled against forming personal attachments to her subjects. Often, those she studied had evoked empathy, sympathy, caring, love...lust, but she could not. The scientist part succeeded, but the empathetic human part had succumbed a few times. It gave her pride that she had resisted the baser desires.

The robot that had woken Liz and served breakfast worked at the clean-up. Liz did not ask, but it poured another mug of coffee.

"I never expected Earth food and delicious coffee." Liz raised the mug in salute. "You know the way to a girl's heart."

"I hope I do." Anya said, and smirked. "Jewel can replicate most organic substances. We had wondered if we got the combinations right, but the databases for the organic generators are large. Contact with Ted's species has brought much of Earth to us. I did not realize coffee was a sexual stimulant."

"You could open a roadside diner for humans," Liz smiled, sipped and the professional Liz tried to ignore the reference to romance.

"But we aren't at the end of the universe," Anya grinned. Liz wondered about how much obscure human culture trivia Anya knew. This brief exchange with Anya sounded a bit like RoH's antics on Earth.

"Thank God," Liz smiled, "but luckily you share this galactic back-water with our solar system. Earth and Jewel are convenient neighbours."

Too convenient? Liz wondered inwardly.

"Coffee stimulates, and meeting for coffee is a common courtship ritual." Liz continued. "Have you tried coffee?"

God, I sound like an anthropologist and a mindless teen...

"Sharing this part of the galaxy with you humans has proven to be good for me," Anya eyed Liz, "and I would like to try coffee, perhaps soon. What can I show you today?"

"Everything," Liz said, "I want to see and know everything."

"That will take more than a day, and much coffee." They laughed.

"My dad used to say that when we went to a new place to check the lay of the land and know your way home. I kept that as my field research rule. I love the forest, but it hides so much. Take me to a high hill where I can see the horizon."

As they walked, Liz noted the gentle slope had no outcropping of rock or loose boulders. No glaciers had plowed into this place. Jewel not only had no seasons, but it had never experienced an ice age. Liz felt newness wherever she looked. Earth's entire surface reflected millions, if not billions, of years of geomorphologic torment. Jewel appeared to be in its youth.

They wandered through the trees without undergrowth or a distinct path. The easy incline seemed intentionally smooth. Liz had travelled through many landscapes on Earth, from deserts, river valleys, jungles and glacial countryside. They had a dynamic jumble, and certainly difficult walking, but Jewel seemed to have an ageless smoothness to it, even more so than the Australian outback. In addition, no wildlife had appeared until birds sang part way up the hill.

"Why are you stepping so carefully?" Anya asked. She walked without care.

"I'm used to seeing snakes, salamanders, or other critters."

"Oh," Anya seemed surprised, "I'm sure they are here and we just can't see any."

Not too far along, a mouse scampered away from the women's feet.

A small furry creature scurried from the trees.

"A chipmunk," Liz said, and then frowned. "This should be on Earth, not Jewel."

"Oh, I love these little ones," Anya said and ignored Liz' upset. "They are my friends."

Anya extended her hand, and the little animal hopped into her palm. She lifted it up, and it found a perch on her shoulder. It had no fear. Anya glanced at Liz. She felt guilt at her deception. Anya had never seen a chipmunk before this minute, but the small creature had an interesting mind.

"Let's go. It gets steeper now," Anya said, and skirted around a first rock outcrop that appeared to be crystal pillows. Liz thought it might have been pure quartzite but it had an extruded, almost toothpaste-look to it. She had loved a woman in university who majored in geology. They could go nowhere without her friend identifying the rocks.

Grad school and careers had separated her from that love. Regrets lingered, and in the longing. Liz contemplated Anya with a mix of professional and personal interest.

"This is all crystal," Liz said.

"This rock is why we call the planet Jewel," Anya said.

"Is it quartzite?"

"We have another name for the rock. It is hard."

Liz wore her grandmother's engagement ring on her right hand. She knelt and used the diamond to scratch a rounded outcrop. It left no mark.

A diamond should scratch quartz, she thought, *and how can this hard bedrock produce soil for the plants?*

Liz frowned.

"Maybe I could get a bit of a souvenir." Liz said.

Anya frowned. "We do no mining on Jewel and don't collect stones."

"Earth kids wouldn't do well here, then." Liz said. Anya looked puzzled.

The surface gave way to rounded bedrock with moss in the hollows. The air held more freshness than the forest floor had at the cabin. They struggled up the steeper grade and came to a peak, well above the tops of the tallest trees. The rock had a hard smooth roundness that reminded Liz of the basalt lava flows her old girlfriend had shown her. A breeze comforted them after the exertion.

Liz swept the horizon and absorbed the beauty. In the near distance, curtains of rain showered beneath puffy clouds. Far off, Liz saw the blue of open water and beyond, jagged mountain peaks rose from the cobalt sea. The sun now had an angle that glinted from off the far-away mountains, and they shone like diamonds.

"It is a jewel," Liz said, "and beautiful."

"We like it," Anya smiled. "The rock shines for us."

"The surface here is gentle, but those look like the most rugged mountains on Earth. They are usually in ranges. We saw those crystal islands from space."

"There are many clusters like this all around Jewel," Anya said. "We think that pressure from below has forced them up. Their sharpness is unusual."

"I would love to go there sometime."

"We don't go near those places," Anya said. "It is uninteresting and dangerous. We are forbidden."

"Who forbids you? Have you visited those larger islands, the little continents?"

"Oh, never," Anya gushed. "They are far away and no Oshki live there. We should never go there.

"It is forbidden." Anya repeated.

Anya had given the explanation and warning too quickly. While she tried to avoid being demanding of the locals while doing fieldwork, Liz took the prohibition as a challenge. She looked at Anya and then back to the crystal teeth on the horizon and she wondered.

"That is not how tectonics works on Earth. Those other continents are a puzzle. Who forbids travel to those places?" Liz asked once more.

Anya hugged Liz.

"I see you have some discomfort. I will not enter your mind unless you want, but perhaps I could help."

"Maybe you can do that to me later," Liz said, "but I would let Ellie, or her daughter RoH, read my mind, even though I never met them on Earth."

"Yes," Anya said, "I met them here, briefly, long ago; they are special. RoH is unique. I will respect your wishes."

"Thank you. Ted reads my thoughts, but he loves Siglinde, and we trust him. He spent many years on Earth."

"Yes, lovers feel safe with one another and if they truly love, they can share everything." Anya touched Liz shoulder. "I wish you could feel safe enough to share with me."

"Look there." She pointed far over the forest where a gigantic bird circled, drifting on unseen breezes, and gradually wandered towards them. It soon came close as an Earthly golden eagle. The creature stooped behind trees and then raised high with what looked like a rabbit in its claws.

Jewel looks more like Earth all the time. Liz thought.

"This is an unfamiliar sight for me." Anya trembled.

Liz felt the warmth of Anya's hand on her shoulder. She did not think the woman tried to seduce her, but it seemed the planet tried. Liz thought of a stage set that began as bare bones but gradually had detail added as the director and crew thought of little embellishments in response to audience wishes. She looked down to the smooth crystalline surface beneath their feet.

Why do I think of a manufactured terrazzo floor? But, it's harder than diamond.

Liz knelt and felt the smooth surface and found it warm even in a shaded spot.

Anya drew her to standing and turned to look at the vista where the sun had risen. A smooth curved line had climbed above the horizon and seemed like a computer graphic of a planet from a movie. The arch, tinted golden with a blue fringe, spanned half of the horizon.

"That is Mother, rising." Anya said. She did not express reverence, as if the planet that held Jewel in its gravitational grip had a mystical significance. Mother sounded matter-of-fact, too much like a simple label.

Is there some sort of origin myth related to that planet? Liz thought.

"That is the mass that Jewel orbits," Anya said, "so it is like a celestial mother. It and Jewel move together around our sun. We have one theory that suggests Jewel split off the mother billions of years ago, but we have no evidence. Mother is too massive, her gravity too strong for anyone to visit. Not even star travellers want to make that trip, so we don't know what Mother is made from.

"Like Earth and the Moon," Liz said. "Do you have poets who write about your dance with Mother? On Earth, the moon brings out imagery and artistic meaning beyond the scientific reality. It is the focus of romantic verse."

Liz eyed her new friend.

"Oh, yes, we have many singers, dancers, and poets here," Anya said. That is one of our major activities, since the mechanicals do all the essential physical work. "I compose a bit, as do all the people. The machines work and we think, create and sing."

Anya sweetly sang.

Mother rose into the sky
To bless my sweet long day
And through to eventide on high
My friend, it longed to stay.

"Did you write that?" Liz asked.

"Just now," Anya said. "It is unsatisfactory, but I will refine it later."

"Jewel sounds like one big hippy commune." Liz laughed.

Anya searched for the reference in her mind.

"We think and discuss serious things too, the stars, the galaxy... the universe and its meaning."

"I would love to be part of that." Liz said. "It is more in Siglinde's field, but I want to visit those beautiful mountains."

Liz noticed Anya's frown. The Crystal Mountains seemed to hold some danger, or secret. Liz loved to solve secrets, and that was why she ended up hunting aliens on Earth. She relished the irony that, on the planet Jewel, she was the alien.

"I want to spend a lot of time with you, and we will discuss many things," Anya's face flushed in the cool breeze. "I do not know if we will visit the Crystal Mountains. Ted and Siglinde are already involved, but you and I will explore together. I am having an abode constructed near yours."

"Why don't you just move into the other room in mine? We could have lots of midnight chats." Liz said.

She felt nervous, hopeful.

"That would be more efficient." Anya said. "Efficiency is a good place to start."

Both laughed and shared the nervousness.

"I hope I can talk with Ted and Siglinde about it," Liz said. "We have been sharing for many years."

"In due time," Anya said, "when you all know more. They will learn from Pater and Mater. You will be mine. Come, let us descend for lunch. Take my hand, and I'll help you pass this hard bit."

Anya held Liz' hand as they leisurely wandered to the cottage.

Chapter 5

The old man

Try to see the world from the eyes of an old man! Old eyes are a good place to begin with for understanding the truths!
- Mehmet Murat Ildan

The man, dressed in comfortable loose coveralls, approached; he looked to be late, middle-aged or older, but Ted could not penetrate the shield hiding the stranger's thoughts. Ted frowned. Aliens like Ted were not used to a mind blocking them. The people of Jewel had power that had to be ancient; however, Jewel seemed to be young and fresh.

"I am Pater," the man said, but did not acknowledge that he had blocked Ted. The star travellers only separated their mind to prevent noisy confusion. They never did it for long and the blocker always made it known that they had separated. It was a courtesy and an essential part of trust; its origins lost in the mists of time, from before they travelled the stars. Shielding suggested secrets, and if there was one taboo among the stars, it was on the keeping of secrets from the community. Mental communication had developed parallel to the simplest technology like the quantum energy devices. Mental connection had become so commonplace in Species 2 that silence in thought upset them all. Anya had been open. Ted examined Pater in the usual star traveller's way of dispassionate curiosity and the slight did not annoy him.

Dressed comfortably, Ted thought and looked at his shoes, *not for work but more like a walk in a park. He is agile, perhaps not as old as he looks.*

"Hello," Siglinde smiled. They could discuss Ted's doubts later. Siglinde felt friendliness in this strange land was her best protection, even if she felt no fear.

The old man stared at Siglinde and smiled. His face had the same coppery hue as Anya's skin. Unlike her flowing dark hair, he cropped his white hair short, and that highlighted his dark, piercing eyes.

"Siglinde, you know RoH," he said. Siglinde read his look as one of reverent admiration.

For RoH, she wondered. It seemed incongruous that his old man, his age implying wisdom, should have reverence for a child such as RoH.

"How,"...

"She left her mark in your brain. She kept you safe. Yes, I love her. My age is of indifferent concern." The man said.

"Are you humanoid as you seem to be?" Siglinde asked.

He and Anya look human, Siglinde thought, *but he read my mind.*

"Mostly," he said, but added no more.

"I am Ted," a hand extended.

"Pater Oosan," the Jewelian shook, "but you are Species 2 appearing as a human with an Earth honorific."

"Let's just say I wanted to blend in," Ted gave Siglinde a one-armed hug.

Pater watched the exchange of loving looks. Of course, he knew the truth, but it gave pleasant feelings to observe this love between these two species. It mimicked similar connections and wise decisions millennia before.

"Your skin is the same colour as Anya's," Siglinde said.

"Anya Mater Ogiin or also Anya Pater Odaanisan is my daughter."

"You have different last names and she has two." Siglinde said.

"We don't use names to identify family. Everyone knows who we are. The secondary names represent our relationship with each other and I mention them to help you. I have many children, and all names end in Pater Odaanisan, Pater Ogozisan, Pater Ningozis or even Pater Akina Gegoo. I am the oldest male here on Jewel, and thus the honorific Oosan. My mate, who you will meet, is Mater Ogiin, the oldest mother."

"We track generations through the mother, so Anya is more commonly, Anya Mater Ogiin, after her mother. Here we all assume the honorific, so you will always know her as Anya and me as Pater."

Siglinde nodded. The names with their link to ancient Earth meant nothing to the physicist. Siglinde resolved to discuss it with Liz.

If Siglinde had met Dawn Waasnodae on Earth, she would have been more puzzled. The names would have excited Dawn, and if she were here, RoH would find missing puzzle pieces.

Liz, the human anthropologist with her knowledge of ancient languages, would understand. Pater thought. *We must keep her from knowing this naming until it is time.*

Pater's thought went to Anya.

On Jewel, Mater Ogiin paralleled, on a shorter time scale, the role of Elsie, one of the ancient Species 2 galactic matriarchs, who now served as a cook and mentor on the Earth bound Goderich farm. In time, Siglinde would meet other inhabitants of Jewel with the last name, Mater Ogiin. She would discover that the honorific applied to subsequent generations that had originated with Mater and Pater. All other individuals that Siglinde encountered had the last name of Mater Aki. Only when once more chatting with RoH Siglinde would understand. That opportunity to meet RoH remained far into the future.

"You also look human. Is that an act?" Siglinde barely kept her scepticism out of her voice. Pater felt it in her mind.

"That is true in this sector and is no act. This is my true self, as is Anya's," Pater said. "You will find other sentient inhabitants elsewhere with different human appearance. I may guide you to them someday. Jewel is special that way."

"I would like to meet them," Siglinde said. "Ted, love, did you know this?"

"We have visited, but we have not met the others. Pater and Anya appear to have abilities, perhaps above those of Ellie. We learned on previous visits that we should leave the agenda to the people here. They will introduce the planet to us as they see fit. That's why I have not warned you."

"Anya has greater ability than Ellie." Siglinde said.

"Perhaps," Ted frowned, "perhaps there is an enhancement on Jewel that does not exist on Earth. No one matches RoH."

Siglinde caught wistfulness in Ted's tone, as if he, a powerful alien, longed for whatever ability the young alien-human hybrid named RoH controlled. Pater's eyes betrayed the same yearning. Ted's community was not the only species of star travellers who held that desire. Siglinde shared the desire, but she knew no living human could aspire to such heights.

I wish I could live to see it. She thought.

"You never know, my love. You may." Ted said. He had followed his lover's thoughts. "I think there are many things to happen in your life that we cannot expect."

"I agree," Pater said. He knew Siglinde had already received some of the benefit of Jewel. They had made no decision how far she would progress. He and the community agreed with Species 2 that events on Earth would determine if humans could also reach the stars. If humans decided wisely, Siglinde had a future role on that planet. If not, she might remain in the stars and perhaps return to Jewel. They had decided nothing. Humans were the rogue factor in the equation, but the Earth species held a galactic importance that all other sentient star-travellers understood.

Ted thought that perhaps the Oshki could only allow any visitor to know what they wanted. He sent the question to the ship that orbited above.

Pater observed the alien's conversation and felt their thoughts. *They and my Oshki have much to learn and will in due time. That is up to RoH, and that is up to Earth.*

It amazed Siglinde that she had known aliens existed and they lived on Earth, but she had not understood what that meant, or where it would lead her or the Earth she loved. Siglinde looked past Pater to the cool, inviting forest and wondered if this was what RoH meant when she said that Siglinde would again wander into the forest.

Could RoH have known, even then? Siglinde wondered. *She visited here before.*

"RoH, as you call her, loved Jewel, and Jewel loved her." Pater said. "I'm sorry for intruding, but your mind is hard to resist. The more you use it, the more it will grow. Being part of Jewel will help. It is a gift Jewel will give to you, as it has done to us and the Oshki. RoH will return soon."

"You guard your mind from me," Ted said, "but Anya does not."

Pater nodded, but said nothing. Pater knew they could trust Species 2, but events must unfold in due time. Slow lessons had more power than sudden revelation.

Siglinde startled. *Pater differentiated himself from the Oshki.*

"Is that a prediction about RoH?" Siglinde asked Pater.

"It is a known and has already been decided." Pater said and pointed to a path through the trees. "Let's walk."

Pater Oosan effortlessly strode into the forest. Ted and Siglinde hurried behind. In contrast to the quiet lack of birds and animals that Siglinde had first observed, the woods overflowed with calling birds. Little critters resembling earthly squirrels and rodents scurried around in fearless company to the visitors. Siglinde could not recall such activity in the Earth forests, but then she mostly visited deliberate parks or remote places with shy animals. Anya had said they let the planet determine its form, so she assumed that this place had changed over eons.

Scientists do not assume, Siglinde reminded herself.

Siglinde felt the peace that cleared her mind. She hummed a tune seemingly from childhood memory and her questioning mind.

> *There was a crooked man, and he went a*
> *crooked mile,*
> *He found a crooked sixpence against a*
> *crooked stile;*
> *He bought a crooked cat, which caught a*
> *crooked mouse,*
> *And they all lived together in a little crooked*
> *house.*

But there is something, and scientific doubt replaced Siglinde's short-lived peace.

They burst from the trees onto a meadow that flanked a bubbling brook. Water fell in a thin stream from the great height of a cliff to their left and made pleasing music as it tumbled onto the rocks below. As with all the planet Jewel, these stones were of some form of almost pure but smoky quartz. Water rang the stones in musical harmony as the slight breeze directed the water fall onto different sized rocks. Siglinde thought of wind chimes, and she felt the peace as if the planet soothed her. The pleasing sequence of notes appeared as if following a score. Despite knowing that the wind must be random, Siglinde could believe that Jewel played a rocky glockenspiel. She wondered if the mathematical purity of earth music applied to other species in the galaxy, or, the thought unsettled, they had arranged this to please human visitors. Whatever the reason, the melody and musical timber relaxed Siglinde.

Pater found a dry bench upwind from the gentle breeze that drifted the misty spray from the falls. Unlike much of what Siglinde had seen here, other than the forest itself, the bench appeared to be old and well used and contrasted the new construction of their cottage.

"I have this thinking place, and I come here often," Pater said, "but also it is a place to talk."

"What do you think and discuss?" Siglinde asked.

"Everything," Pater said. "Mostly, we wonder about the nature and the meaning of the universe. We find the remaining unanswered questions to be profound and hard."

"I think I never know all the questions, let alone the answers." Siglinde said.

Pater stared at Siglinde.

I see now why we are so interested in the human species. Pater thought.

"I think that's our situation, too." Pater said.

"How long have you been doing this? Do you understand the evolution of your species, and why don't you go into the galaxy?" Siglinde asked.

"That's many questions," Pater frowned. "We have wondered about that, and have as few answers as we do for our origins, the meaning of life and the true nature of the cosmos.

"Human physics and galactic science agree on the basic energy rules. That energy can neither be created nor destroyed raises the fundamental question: how can the universe exist? We think we can find the answer, but at the moment no one, human or star species, has the data to do it."

"That sounds vague. To me, your minds are overpowering. I find it hard to believe you don't have those answers sorted out." Siglinde said.

"Oshki collective memory is about one thousand Earth years. Our minds have always been this way. We understand it is genetic, and we have measured ourselves. Our genes differ in individuals, but are surprisingly of the same mixture. Our minds seem powerful to you, and you do not share that ability because you are missing one of those genetic components that alter the brain. The other genes we share with you."

"How do you know that?" Siglinde asked. Pater had not differentiated himself from the Oshki, but

Siglinde had her doubts. Comparing Pater to Anya, Siglinde saw this old man as having more confidence and freedom to speak than Anya had.

"Anya took the measure of you a few minutes after you arrived. We find your genetics fascinating."

Siglinde remembered Anya having described her and Liz as "Nova species, pure variant human."

"So, where did your other genes come from?" Siglinde asked.

"We don't know." Pater did not want to be devious, but these visitors would discover the disparity in the Oshki at the right time. They would then understand his and Mater's special place and that including himself and Mater as part of the Oshki was only partly true. For the humans, and even Ted of Species 2, to know too much, too soon, would skew the results of their intended observation. In due time, of course, they would draw these visitors and many more into the effort and Pater and Mater would reveal all. Anya had informed him of Liz's curiosity about the Crystal Mountains, and Pater thought it likely that Liz's pushiness might hurry the timetable. The relatively short lifespans of humans made them more impatient than star travellers of all species.

"It fascinated us," Pater said. "Ellie, RoH's mother has a similar but weaker mixture and of course is from nova humans and your species," he turned to Ted. "RoH has a similar mixture, but it seems she is even more complete but different from ours. We hope to understand RoH more completely, but in that effort, we require her permission."

"We have an unproved idea that Jewel gave us the genetics to be what we are, mentally, and we will observe to see if species Nova-1," he stared at Siglinde, "will show signs of that growth. We have a theory that thinking changes the mind physically, and that is how sentient species eventually can function at the quantum level. Perhaps Jewel strengthens that. Actually, I know that just being on Jewel leads to synaptic morphing and perhaps genetic enhancement in mature individuals."

"It is also an enigma why RoH seems above us, but we speculate her mother, Ellie, had some importance in that. With all of this emphasis on genetics, we forget that nurturing has an important place in development. Contact with humans taught star travellers that truth. RoH seems to be all of her mother, both genes and nurture, and more than her mother of your species too, Ted, but she has a factor none of us possess."

Once more, Pater tried not to feel bad in deception. He knew of the exact physical reality of the entity that called herself, RoH. Why this had led to unexpected results challenged the best minds of the galactic collective. The star travellers had retreated to the consideration of Ellie's influence during RoH's development, but it satisfied no one without proof, and that data seemed elusive.

"You think you are hybrids?" Ted asked.

"Yes, but not with your species," Pater stared at Ted and felt more comfortable approaching nearer to the truth while extending the lie. "One thing I hope for is that you and Siglinde may spark some progress on that question. There are many Oshki clamouring to meet you both, and Liz, too."

Once more, Pater felt some guilt at delaying the truth.

"I think, therefore I evolve." Siglinde smiled. Her stomach growled. Sigma D had climbed high into the sky, and its light made fleeting rainbows in the mists of the waterfall.

"Oh, I'm sorry, you must be hungry and thirsty," Pater said.

A robot appeared and Siglinde first thought Art had arrived. The automaton carried a large container of unfamiliar material.

"I am not AR64-T, Art, as you call your helper. I am AR64-N. AR64-T awaits your return to your abode."

"I'll call you Arn, then," Siglinde smiled. She could not tell if the machine expressed pleasure or confusion at her humanizing.

"Arn, as you call it, is my personal helper, although we own nothing." Pater said. "Arn is a helper to all, as is your Art unit. They are identical in every way, as are all bi-pedal Omni-service units, and could switch roles without you knowing. That won't happen, of course." Pater said. In fact, that your interactions have modified the Art machine's self-awareness fascinates us.

Arn unpacked a lunch. Actually, the container gyrated and formed a table in front of the bench. A plate of some strange food went to Pater and two plates bearing hot schnitzel and baked potatoes appeared for Ted and Siglinde. Siglinde found the food identical to what her grandmother once served. Goblets of cool white wine came from the same space.

"I told you we would have a waterfall and good food on our honeymoon," Ted laughed. He balanced a bit of meat on his fork. Earlier alien visitors to Earth could not really eat Earth food, but only because of its unfamiliarity. RoH's great-great-grandfather suffered because of it. When they had long-term assignments such as Ted's, they learned to consume and digest Earth meals.

"I guess I can trust you then," Siglinde kissed Ted on the cheek.

Siglinde had become used to alien energy manipulation and felt no surprise that hot and cold could have come from the same space and seemed to defy the rules of heat flow. The laws of thermodynamics seemed to be more observation and less law.

"We don't change the laws," Pater smiled at her, "and we can only do things like that in limited space and time. As you see, now the laws apply and your food cools and the drinks become warm. Please, eat."

"What is that you are eating?" Siglinde savoured her feast and eyed what appeared to be a vegetarian delight before Pater.

"It is from the natural abundance of Jewel," Pater said. "While you enjoy animal protein, the planet provides us with its equivalent, along with various other vegetable gifts. They yield a healthy diet. We understand that other planets have evolved other ways, such as Earth has for its species."

"On earth, you would be called vegans." Siglinde said.

Pater paused, stared, and Siglinde felt a feather's touch.

"It is interesting that there is a conflict on Earth over diet. Arguing over these things, food differences seems strange to us. The millions of years of evolution of species there has given a large diversity of species and each has differing or parallel food sources, mainly eating each other as we do the plants here. That seems simply the natural order and whether one chooses one species to consume is not a point to argue. We honour the sacrifice of all species for our use."

"Some humans think that if other humans don't follow their beliefs or actions, they challenge or diminish them. That often leads to fighting." Siglinde savoured each delicious bite.

Again, she felt a feather's touch.

"Hmm," Pater seemed to think, "Nova Species Human is a strange mixture of competitiveness and cooperation. It is no doubt because of your evolution and something needed for success as a species. You have now reached the point of either choosing the cooperative over conflict or allowing conflict to exterminate you. Lacking a superior predator, humans have become their own worst enemy. Sad, interesting, but sad..."

"That's another thing humans fight about," Siglinde laughed.

"It is why Ellie and more so RoH are important to Earth. RoH, of course, has importance to the galaxy." Pater smiled as if the thought of RoH cheered him.

"In what way...?" Siglinde asked.

"She bridges a deficiency in us," Pater said.

"I didn't think you had any shortcomings," Siglinde replied.

"What we know of ourselves, of our thousand year existence is that we have evolved and sit somewhere between Ellie and RoH, but we don't know if we need to evolve into versions of RoH, or, now that she exists, if that is necessary. Oshki thought that our purpose was to evolve into a new galactic population and we had to wait for the right time to go into the galaxy. RoH's existence makes us question that idea."

Pater and Mater and the collective they represented had concluded that the development of RoH had made Jewel redundant. No one could imagine that they would abandon Jewel, but perhaps they would repurpose it.

"For a thousand years, we thought we had a purpose in the cosmos. Now it disquiets us, we may no longer have that reason. It seems to involve RoH. We do not need her to bring peace, so we do not yet understand her role."

"My knowing RoH makes it hard to believe that she has any negative effect on anything." Siglinde said.

"We don't see it as bad; please don't make that mistake; however, we think she, by existing, puts us out of a job. Jewel eagerly awaits her next visit."

"You said Jewel," Siglinde said.

"It is the oneness of Jewel, the whole of the Oshki, that waits. Even the others in the far lands wait, although they live in ignorance."

"Will that be soon? I think she's busy on Earth," Ted said.

Pater stared into the forest and then looked at the majesty of the falling water.

"You will be here to greet her," Pater smiled.

"That had better be soon. I need to get back to mow the lawn." Siglinde laughed.

"Relax, my friend," Pater took her hand. "Your other self is busy helping the president of one of the minor national divisions on your planet to survive a possible fatal crisis. We don't know if they, or you, will be successful."

"RoH has made significant progress in dealing with another crisis, one your species caused," Pater nodded towards Ted. "Once that is done, her being on Earth may not be needed so urgently, and she will then be free to tend to more important affairs of the galaxy. Her mother, along with Species 2, has the resources to accomplish the task there, if that is possible."

"You make it sound as if RoH will be a diplomat unifying the residents of the galaxy." Siglinde said.

"That may be so," Pater said. "We have yet to explore all the vastness of our galactic organism. There is; however, a visitor, a rogue planetary system that comes from the Great companion from the galaxy, humans call Andromeda. If that is so, the best of us must be the greeter, even if she is not yet aware of her mission. It will arrive within range soon."

"RoH," Siglinde asked.

"We believe that there is a sentient, technical species on at least one planet orbiting that travelling star. It interests us to discover if DNA is the basis of their life. Of course, there is the danger that they have not developed enough to be peaceful. If that proves true, then RoH must shield our galaxy. We just don't know."

"RoH may have the ability, but you are interested in Jewel. We should venture out." Pater beckoned Arn, and the machine collapsed the table into the carrier.

"I will return to my Mater now," Pater said, "but we will welcome you tomorrow for a visit. Walk this way when you are ready in the morning. Time has little importance on Jewel."

Pater looked at Ted and Siglinde and felt their questions and doubts.

"We have much to share when it is time. Explore, and follow your questions and doubts," Pater looked at Siglinde. "A scientist must question and explore those issues. You already puzzle about Jewel and the Oshki. No one will hinder you."

Pater turned and walked into the trees without looking back.

"I have a feeling that Jewel is more than it seems." Siglinde said.

CHAPTER 6

Liz's first dream

Dreams are like stars. You may never touch them, but if you follow them, they will lead you to your destiny.
-Liam James

The first dream shook me to the core. I had never dreamed so vividly, and conflict between horror and safety filled the night. Anya gave me a goodnight hug, and we went to our rooms on the first night that we shared the cottage. I slept. I'm not sure how long I dreamed, but it seemed to last the night. Dreams always appear to be long, but our sub-conscious minds can tell a story in seconds what we would need hours to convey awake.

In my understanding, dreaming is simply our minds ordering and filing memories and thoughts of the previous day, or perhaps older. Perhaps we draw from some archetypical collective conscious as some think, and somehow, our brains translate this into a story. The images and events appear as if these memories are sheets of paper scattered on the floor and the mind had read these random pages and spun that content into a tale. It usually makes for a wild ride as the brain united arbitrary disconnected facts along with our recent emotions into a crazy story.

I learned later that on Jewel some dreams come from without. When I woke, I could believe I had gone mad. The memory of the dream remained crystal clear. I soon discovered that the idea of crystal clarity made sense on Jewel. It had brought back the horrible time my family rejected me. I did not yet appreciate the changes developing in my mind or the role of Jewel through Anya. That revelation came later.

A shout..."get out sinner" "but mother"...a door slam...cold...dark...lonely...fear...horror...hopeless... sad...dark...alone...alone...swirling...over...and again...then...

...into the forest...someone is with me...who? Light...comfort...fade...darkness...darkness... somewhere...where?...what...images...diamonds... necklace...no...teeth...snarling...dripping...blood... no...blue...clear...water...the crystal teeth melt... deeper into the dark. Where is my companion? I

need her hand, but I cannot find it. I know she is there, somewhere...searching...reaching. Is she lost and scared like me?

Something chasing, silent evil, I run...heavy legs. It's closer...close. The ground rises...steep hill. I slip, sliding down, a silent scream...dark...weeds grasp my ankles. Lost, I am lost, that time in Borneo, heat, wet, pressing against me, exploding lungs. Tears, tears done.

Suddenly, her hand in mine, pulling me through the tangled brush. We burst into the open. Green shrubs sweep down to a white beach. Waves wash gently on the shore, soothing, and the Crystal Mountains shine beyond the shimmering blue sea, the Crystal Mountains calling in a musical seduction, I must go to the crystals beyond the water, Anya smiles...she says, "I am here; I am here..."

Liz startled awake. Sweat soaked her bed. She sat and looked around. Her trembles eased. A morning bird called through the open window and comforted as if Jewel wished to soothe her. A sudden desire to see the crystal peaks and the shimmering sea consumed her.

A soft knock on her bedroom door broke her trance.

"I am here. You dreamed; come for breakfast," Anya said. Her smile told of two things, Anya's affection and her knowing more than she might of Liz's nighttime horror.

"You are a species of profound power," Liz said.

She and Anya lingered over breakfast. The service robot, AR64-V, or Arv waited patiently at the kitchen doorway.

"I don't understand why you have never developed space travel."

"Our history teaches us patience. The galaxy visits us and has already done so with Species 2, your friend Ted, for instance, RoH and, to my delight, you, Liz. More will come, and our understanding says we came from the stars. We cannot decipher that mystery. It remains a powerful story that Pater and Mater tell that no one here can unravel."

Anya seemed at ease with the unsolved puzzle. The people of Jewel accepted it as an unknowable, but Mater and Pater knew.

"On Earth, we would call that religion," Liz said. "My job on Earth is to understand cultures and especially their myths and origin stories. All seem to involve extra-terrestrial beginnings, usually a deity. When humans do not have information to understand, we satisfy our deep need to know by making up stories to explain. Many insist on believing the stories even after evidence gives a more correct explanation. Is that what you have on Jewel?"

"It differs, I think. On Earth, most of your religions advocate some sort of exceptional place for your species. Oshki have none of that in our belief. We know universal processes made us, but in our particular place, there seems to have been an intermediate entity. We detect a strange genetic structure that suggests we have a two species origin."

"You are hybrids like Ellie and RoH are combinations of Species 2 and humans?"

"We might assume that is one, perhaps the best possibility." Anya said. "We detect one part of our genetics is like Nova Species, Human." Anya stared at Liz. "Somewhat like yours, but not exactly. The other is not, as far as we might tell, Species 2."

"So that may be why RoH intrigues you so much."

"Yes, Mater and Pater did the analysis. They told us RoH is clearly Species 2 and human." Anya said. She never questioned that Mater and Pater might choose to reveal only part of the story.

"RoH's greater potential than ours fascinates us. We do not know why, even though Mater and Pater examined her in every detail at the one time she visited. Her genetics appear to be a combination making a completely new species, not human, not Species 2, and certainly not us to our other part."

"The name her Species 2 family gave her partially means giver of new life. Perhaps that is more correct than they knew. RoH is definitely unique."

Liz contemplated Anya. The simple acceptance of these possibilities without prejudice contrasted with much of humanity's bigoted reaction to the existence of any alien species from the stars. Some humans held so strongly to their creation myths that they would die to protect the stories.

Earth has a long way to go, Liz thought.

"It comes from our understanding that we are not special in the universe." Anya had peeked into Liz's thoughts, "oh, I'm sorry, I did not mean to spy."

"If we are to have a good relationship," Liz said, "I think you should not do that. I find you attractive as a friend, but how can I trust you if you know all of me and my thoughts and feelings, and I know nothing of yours? Solid relationships depend on trust."

"I find you attractive too," copper skin hid Anya's blush, "and would want our relationship to continue, so I will refrain. Please trust that I will not violate you or betray you. We think your mind will grow, change with Jewel's help, and we will come to know each other on even terms."

"Thank you." Liz took Anya's hand across the table. "My thoughts are often preliminary and don't reflect my genuine feelings or doubts. My science training requires that I question, doubt, examine and propose many hypotheses that most often end up being wrong. I wouldn't want any of my thoughts about you and Jewel to hurt our togetherness."

"On Jewel," Anya said, "we find guarding minds is not too helpful for trust and bonding, but you cannot be in me, at least not yet, and that is unfair. Bonding at our level requires a two-way flow. I hope you will share your feelings and thoughts often, but I will leave that to you. Here we share even poorly formed ideas and thoughts as if they are just discussion, not positions to be defended. If one of us becomes stubborn, most of the rest will gang up on the person with many counter arguments. It's tedious and we don't do it lightly or often."

"I'll try to tell all," Liz' dark skin hid the sudden warmth in her cheeks. It worried her more that Anya might read her emotions, her attitude to their friendship before Liz even understood her feelings.

Her mind was one thing; her heart was dangerous territory.

What did Anya mean by bonding? Liz wondered.

"You know what I would really like," Liz said, "is to visit those crystal mountains. Earth has nothing like that."

"I will take you," Anya seemed eager and to have forgotten her original position, Jewel forbid such a trip. She knew the fear and desire that had consumed Liz in dreaming. Anya's change of heart had come to her in the night. Jewel had given dreams to both her and Liz, but Anya did not know why Jewel might now want Liz to reach the Crystal Mountains. She had interrogated Pater in the night, and he had agreed to the trip, but they were not to travel too soon.

"There's a community of wise ones that lives on the shore opposite the nearest island. We call them the guardians of Jewel. They do not have any special power or ability beyond ours, but our history says they are where our species first appeared. My Pater and Mater are of those, and we are the children of Mater and Pater. Since then, we have spread over the entire continent, even into the more remote and hostile regions."

"It is a long walk. I will arrange for our comfort along the path."

"You don't have aeroplanes or trains here?"

"We are never in a hurry," Anya replied. "You and I have no reason to hurry. The time is not yet for that. Information travels instantaneously and we only visit a place physically to learn. We don't need that, but we don't know the Crystal Mountains either."

"What, you never get together just to have a beer?" Liz laughed.

"Explain, please," Anya frowned. I won't read your thoughts.

"Conviviality," Liz replied, "just to get together to enjoy being with someone and have fun. On Earth it usually means sitting round some neutral place. Some are called pubs where we share drinks, beer being the most common, and we just enjoy each other's company."

"Oh, we constantly get together to have fun," Anya said. This time, Anya's burnished cheeks betrayed her blush.

"We do not consume alcohol, though. It's bad for both the mind and the body."

Liz pretended not to notice the fire in Anya's face. Perhaps conviviality on Jewel involved more than a long neck and pretzels and involved more intimacy.

Chapter 7

Siglinde spins a spoon

"Why, sometimes I've believed as many as six impossible things before breakfast."
- Alice's Adventures in Wonderland

While Liz suffered through the horror and happiness of her dream, Siglinde spent an uneasy night. She woke several times. Her mind would not shut up from asking questions. Ted found her sitting at the kitchen table as dawn broke. Art had appeared immediately and offered Siglinde breakfast. She had shooed him away, but he would return soon to make breakfast.

Siglinde's serious expression did not surprise Ted. He had seen that look frequently at NAAP headquarters on earth, and he knew she had a scientific problem running in her head. Siglinde had not had that stare since she had discovered the reality of Ellie Keys and RoH. Ted entered her thoughts.

"Yes, it's a frustrating mystery," Ted said.

"I'm not a geologist," Siglinde said, "but the bedrock here seems to be a quartzite and nothing else. That would be rare, almost like discovering a planet of pure gold or only any other mineral. It looks like Earth, but Earth is a more complex ball of minerals and tectonic dynamics that Jewel lacks. The surface reflects the interior.

"The spin and lack of axial tilt to orbital inclination are too convenient and keep the face of the planet normal to the flow of radiation from Sigma Draconis. Why has the star not baked the place dry and irradiated it? I would expect violent air flow and ocean currents to carry the equatorial het to the pole, but Jewel, at least its atmosphere, seems quiet and ideal. We haven't been here long enough to know about the oceans. The heat budget here seems contrived as if there is some sort of planetary air conditioner. Along with that, the rotation makes days almost twenty-four Earth hours long.

"Where does the water come from? Most of Earth's water hides deep in the crust and mantel and came from the early bombardment of icy bodies. Volcanoes expel water from that remaining deep source. Have your people detected any craters or other impact features?"

"No," Ted said, "and you are repeating questions we have struggled with."

"Tectonic forces, except for a few exceptions, eradicate impact craters on Earth over a few hundred million years." Siglinde said. "Bodies like the moon, Mars and other moons and planets with no molten core have many scars billions of years old. If Jewel has a solid core, why are there no visible impact craters? Jewel seems like a virgin world.

"I wish I had a lab and satellite data sets." Siglinde said, and then she smiled. "I have an idea."

Siglinde rummaged in a drawer and pulled out a ball of string. This did not surprise her. Siglinde already suspected that her mind had designed and furnished the cottage.

"This is what I had at home in my junk drawer," she said and retrieved a spoon. She pulled her shirt open and stood in her bra.

"Whoa, you are tempting," Ted said. "Let's get busy."

"Down, lover boy, this is science at work." Siglinde stroked the spoon with a button from her blouse.

"These buttons are magnetic closures," she said. "The magnets are small but strong." Her hand flew over the spoon as the button rasped against the metal and made the spoon into a compass needle. Siglinde counted down from 100.

"That should be enough." She tied the string to the spoon and held it above the table, so that the spoon sat unmoving and let go. It slowly rotated until it pointed at the bedroom door.

"It's telling us something," Ted laughed. Siglinde frowned with science, not sex on her mind.

"That's the orientation to the magnetic field, but it isn't the north pole of Jewel."

The spoon suddenly rotated once more. It pointed to another spot.

"Wow, what the…?" Siglinde asked. "I didn't do that. It shouldn't have happened."

Siglinde's eyes flashed in scientific curiosity.

"Okay, alien genius, what's your explanation?"

Ted stared at the crude compass and frowned. "Damned if I know."

"It rotated about 30 degrees on its own," Siglinde said.

She tied the string to an upper cupboard door handle and drew a line on the countertop to record the direction. They waited. The spoon rotated, more slowly this time, but rested some angle off. Siglinde marked the counter, and again the spoon moved unaided, and once more until she had arrows pointing in several directions in an almost circular sweep.

"The pole changes rapidly," she said. "I don't understand." She searched in vain for some learning that would help.

"Large bodies with a super-ice core can have unstable magnetic fields," Ted said. "Perhaps…"

"Jewel has a core of solid ice," Siglinde finished. "How can that be?"

"You aren't an astrophysicist," Ted said. "In your solar system, Uranus and Neptune have strange, multi-polar magnetic fields. It is because water at the pressures inside them makes a strange, high-temperature ice. We star travellers can do that by manipulating structures without the pressures. I can't see how Jewel could have those conditions, either natural or deliberate. Jewel is just too small for that to happen naturally. We make similar structures by manipulating metal into normal temperature superconductors as part of our quantum electricity generators, but they are small compared to a planet and not made of ice. The ship we travelled on had one the size of an Earth house. For us, that's big. Our quantum manipulation could not build an Earth-size core of water super-ice. We observed the dynamic polarity from above, but had little data to conclude anything."

"A body this large should have a molten core from radioactivity, unless..." Siglinde's voice trailed off. "Unless it's made of no radioactive minerals, and that would be weird. But how does that magnetic field deflect solar and cosmic rays? Nothing should be alive here."

"Art," Siglinde called, and the robot appeared from its resting place.

"Art, I want a little laboratory scale, accurate to four decimal places, metric please. You may enter my mind for the details."

Art stared and departed in silence. Ted manoeuvred Siglinde to the couch for a little smooching. He already knew that his lover did her best thinking when she relaxed. Art's quick return ended the intimacy.

Art placed a silver-coloured metal device on the kitchen table. It had a digital readout that gave Siglinde five decimal places of accuracy.

"Metric," Siglinde asked.

"Yes," Art said, "and here are some test weights from one gram to a kilogram. Shall I serve breakfast?"

Siglinde took the 100 gram mass and calibrated the machine. There was no need. The factory settings were accurate to the last decimal. Every test mass gave the same accuracy. It impressed her. She took a small electronic pad and noted the place, time, and result. Siglinde always considered a zero to be a valid data point. The scale, the 100 gram weight and the magnetized spoon went into a small backpack. She was ready to explore.

Ted did not need to ask. His and Siglinde's minds shared. She intended to check the variations in Jewel's gravity and magnetic field as they travelled, searching for variations in composition deep inside the planet.

Siglinde disappeared out the back door and returned with a handful of soil. The earth ended up in a juice glass. Siglinde found vinegar in the expected cupboard as in her Virginia apartment and flooded the dirt. Small bubbles appeared.

"This soil has lime in it. Where did that come from on a planet that is mostly silicate? I'm no expert, but I don't know how you can make lime from silicate. It's like they went to the garden centre and bought the soil. It's more a garden than a natural landscape."

"Another thing, those shiny islands we saw on the way down looked evenly spaced."

"That's one mystery we could examine from space," Ted said. "There are many of them and they form a regular dodecahedron. We thought it was a tectonic process, but as you said, there are no tectonics here. Jewel has a solid core."

"And a solid mystery," Siglinde said. "I want to talk to Liz. This place gives me the creeps. It's as if it's an illusion, or at least an artefact."

Art arrived with breakfast.

Chapter 8

Dreamer's way

Never go on trips with anyone you do not love.
- Ernest Hemingway

"I want to get going." Liz tried to sound patient, but the intense dream had seized her. She needed to know, to understand. Anya had promised to guide her to the island that held the nearest mountains of crystal, the object of her dream, but the morning had passed while Anya discussed it with distant minds. Liz spent the time updating her journal into her electronic pad.

"I had to plan and get permission from Mater," Anya said. "We have never done this before. It intrigues and challenges us. We must make stops on the way. Many want to meet you. They want to know why you want this, and aliens intrigue us."

"I have a strange feeling about all this," Liz said. "Are we humans the first aliens to visit Jewel, other than Ted's bunch?"

Liz put both hands on Anya's shoulders and looked into her eyes. Anya looked away. Anya did not mention that they wanted to delay.

Mater and Pater wanted to choreograph the travels and discoveries of Liz, Ted and Siglinde. Meeting others would be a cover for a longer, meandering path for Liz that would allow better timing for Siglinde's trip. The shores lay only a half-day's direct walk from the cottage, but Anya counted on Liz not having a good grasp of local geography. It pleased Anya that this meant she had more time with the fascinating Earthling. She did not know why, but it might be the colour of her skin or the exotic attraction of a stranger that raised unfamiliar feelings in Anya. Relationships between Oshki were open because of their mental abilities and sharing. With Liz, it could not be that easy involvement. How to do it gave Anya an unfamiliar problem.

The Oshki had a deep taboo against visiting the islands, and they had allowed it after deliberating the goals of Jewel. Hiding things from anyone, even outsiders, raised a dilemma for the Oshki, who hid nothing from each other. They would delay until what Mater and Pater called the right time. These ancients had guided Jewel forever and no Oshki ever questioned their advice. For Mater and Pater, guiding the Oshki did not include dictating or interfering in daily activities; however, they always planned to introduce humans to the reality of Jewel. That plan was as old as Jewel, and with the appearance of RoH, fulfilling the design became urgent. Developments on Jewel would hopefully contribute to a good outcome on Earth, and by default, give RoH a calm heart and the strength to fulfill her great mission.

Jewel's abundance created such a gentle climate that the Oshki normally required little shelter. Even though they had pleasant structures for rest, many times Oshki would sleep outside and enjoy bathing in the usual gentle night showers.

No inhabitant lacked physical needs, such as food. While many gardened both for food and joy, the bulk of the nourishment came from processes overseen by robots. Only the mechanicals went into the vast underground network of factories and warehouses that serviced the Oshki continent. Siglinde would have found the source of her soil in the depths.

They did not use replicators which would defy the laws of physics, but the food factories hosted sophisticated organic templates to grow whatever foods might be in the data banks. Admittedly, quantum manipulation enhanced the process to hours instead of days or months. The procedure created plant embryos, seeds without the protective husk that then germinated in nutrient baths to produce the plant type needed.

This genetic library hosted examples of diverse galactic life, but they also contained every genetic record from Earth. Full seeds also resulted and the Oshki used them for pleasure gardening. Vats produced animal protein in whatever form required, such as a schnitzel for Siglinde. For all things, vast, millennium old stores of nutrients provided the material needed. When humans arrived, Jewel brought fresh foods from the far continents.

The extensive variety of Earth's organic material allowed Siglinde to eat schnitzel and baked potato, and they all could enjoy coffee and other Earth delights. Human connoisseurs would note differences in taste from the real Earth varieties, but nothing made the food objectionable. A galactic expert on the subject soon would complain that the hot chocolate made on Jewel did not meet Earth standards, and that would instigate a frenzy to gain the real thing.

Ted received a diet that appeared to be from Earth, but the formulations were closer to star-traveller's needs. His decades of playing human on Earth had changed his tastes. Ted's love for Siglinde encouraged an Earthly diet.

The humans provided an interesting necessity and gave the Oshki much to think about. Their first assessment said that modern humans needed the reassurance of walls and closed space. Why that might be so eluded the experience of the Oshki. They knew the old stories, of course, when the first generation of legend on Jewel lived in huts, but those days had long gone if they ever existed. No one had ever thought to venture to the poles where protection from the constant cold would be required. The Oshki lived a more sophisticated version of humans living in the Earth's sub-tropical zones. They experienced no seasons and could not know the requirements for human protection needed at higher latitudes. The climates on the other continents more resembled Earthly uncertainty.

Because Jewel automatically met their needs, the Oshki did not explore the surface or travel in search of food. They normally spent their days in creative ways such as gardening, arts and poetic verse while, no matter what physical activity, their linked minds contemplated the purpose and laws of the universe. Only the occasional desire for shelter from rain led the Oshki to employ the various structures from rounded artificial domes of a durable, moulded plastic material or simple open walled platforms made from local wood with waterproof roofs.

Anya felt guilt at deceiving Liz. She wanted nothing less than a genuine bond with the Earthling woman. Despite the linking of all Oshki's minds, and the viability of all forms of intimate contact, an individual Oshki could still feel loneliness. They had often discussed this and decided that it related to their brain structure and perhaps that required one-on-one personal connection. Reproduction did not require it, and the collective approved of anyone having a baby. Conception usually occurred during an act of physical love between a male and female. They recognized youngsters needed play mates for proper development and the group had a firm idea that the number of children of near the same age must be four. In every small village, all age cohorts comprised at least four Oshki of the nearly same age. Although gestation vats were available, the community preferred that the female carry the child for the 270 days of normal pregnancy. The similarity with humans ended there, with birthing made a less painful experience with the Oshki mental abilities, and then the parents and the community nurtured the child. Developing children felt love and caring from all villagers. Age cohorts held a bond that comforted the individuals and strengthened the community.

They debated the maximum population that would be desirable. They agreed that the Oshki population had not yet reached the ideal, and they added generations at a reasonable pace. In a rare collaboration with the mechanicals, the Oshki discussed resource limits for food. Mater and Pater led the interactions with the robot servants, but the pair knew the situation with resources and recognized there were no meaningful limits. They preferred their Oshki offspring to have worked through the issues as a group.

Many Oshki communities existed on the continent and they all functioned in the same way. Every Oshki knew about the other communities and occasional visits happened. While these appeared to be casual, Mater and Pater made sure that inter-community bonding led to individuals migrating from one village to another, cohabitations and offspring. The senior progenitors had some difficulty in disguising the arrangement from the Oshki, who shared such mental ability that the merest hint would have led to awkward questions. It amazed Mater and Pater that the communities did not notice that almost all these bonds resulted in pregnancies. The goal of genetic diversity should have become obvious.

No one knew why, but deep bonding between individuals required some separation from the whole, and this could be worrying, if not appalling. They felt comfort in the all, but the linked community did not always provide enough. The first time someone disconnected from the all created fear, and doing so had become a rite of passage. It usually formed part of the ritual surrounding puberty. Forming a deep emotional and physical bond with another Oshki of whatever gender needed that scary step. It required a strong emotional desire between individuals, what humans call love, for it to be done amongst adults. Since reproduction did not place high in these situations, gender became meaningless. Lovers would only disconnect for intimate moments and otherwise remained part of them all. The hunger for the comfort of the whole always eventually overrode the need for privacy raised by desire.

"Let's go," Anya said at last.

"Shouldn't we pack supplies?" Liz asked.

It had occurred to her she had none of the normal kit, boots and clothes that she used on any field work. Despite her questions, being on Jewel seemed more of a vacation.

"We lack for nothing," Anya said. "Jewel will take care of us."

"Anya," Arv said aloud, more to include Liz than the need for anything but the mental connection with Anya. AR64-T has sent a request for you two to visit the other human and the Species 2 entity. They have discovered something that they want to share."

"Don't you two make a delightful couple?" Ted greeted Liz and Anya.

Burnished copper and black skin hid blushes. The innocent felt guilt about unacknowledged desires.

"What's up, Doc?" Liz hugged Siglinde.

With the eagerness of a grade 6 presenting her science project, Siglinde showed the spinning spoon and her sketch on the counter.

"Jewel is weird and wonderful," she said.

"Tell me something new." Liz laughed and looked at Anya.

"Why did you do that?" Anya asked Siglinde.

"We are scientists," Liz said. "When we don't understand or know, we experiment."

"What does this mean, Siglinde?"

"Ted thinks Jewel has a solid ice or some type of super-conducting core, perhaps hot like Uranus or Neptune, but under so much pressure, the water behaves like ice, hot ice. The multiple, dynamic poles result from weird electro-magnetic dynamics of that strange material."

"Jewel is too small for that, but these are the facts," Ted said. "The hot ice idea may not be valid, but there are no other hypotheses at the moment. We don't know how pure quartz behaves at the core of large bodies like Jewel."

Anya looked startled.

"We never knew," Anya said. "We just took Jewel to be Jewel. Jewel just is, and as it should be."

"You have never explored Jewel in any way?" Siglinde asked.

"Perhaps Mater and Pater know," Anya said. "They encourage us to be inquisitive and think, but about big questions of the stars, the galaxy, and the universe, not about Jewel. We have created grand theories and mathematic philosophies about it all, but they never suggested we learn about the Jewel under our feet."

"Jewel might be well named," Liz said. "It looks like pure quartzite and is hard, with so signs of weathering, glaciation or anything. Diamond won't scratch it."

"We have done that with quartz," Ted said. "We could reproduce the hardness by quantum manipulation of the crystals, even make them super-conducting, but not on the scale of this planet."

Pater and Mater knew about Siglinde's experiments and Liz's testing the hardness of the bedrock. When they allowed the star travellers to bring the humans, the overseers had not expected scientific minds full of questions and ingenuity. Since they had brought the Oshki progenitors, humans on Earth had advanced more than reports had suggested, and certainly further than the control populations on the other two continents of Jewel. Liz and Siglinde presented an exciting, unintended opportunity for study. Pater and Mater had discussed the possibility that the tight control of Jewel might not produce meaningful results. The concept of Jewel might be obsolete.

The development of the insightful theory by Siglinde, and her star travelling lover, and Liz's persistent questioning pushed the agenda faster than planned.

Events on Earth that they hoped would drive the future on Jewel might have to catch up to fulfil the plan. A cosmic dance had to be choreographed to keep events on Earth and Jewel synchronous.

"We have only explored a small part of the galaxy, but our species has never found a place like Jewel." Ted said.

"I can't see how fertile soil can weather from that sterile bed rock. It requires more than just silica." Siglinde pointed to her glass of dirty water. "The soil is fertile, but it is out of place. I wish I had a lab for full analysis of its metal and organic content."

"Perhaps they will allow me to send samples to the ship." Ted said.

Anya paused and stared at Ted. Art directed his sensors towards her. Siglinde thought she might read something into nothing, but she thought the machine looked distraught.

"Mater and Pater must discuss this with you," Anya said, but a little too abruptly. "Liz and I are going on a journey."

Chapter 9

Chasing the rabbit

"It would be so nice if something made sense for a change."
 — Alice's Adventures in Wonderland

As Liz and Anya headed into the trees, Siglinde and Ted took the path to the waterfall. Beyond that, they followed where Pater had gone the day before.

Siglinde paid close attention to her surroundings and straddled the thin line between suspicion and scientific curiosity. The circumstances of their visit seemed to be too perfect. The layout of the house, too familiar, the sweeping meadow allowing a view of the sky, the food, birds and animals suddenly appearing, all seemed more than a coincidence. She supposed a connection between her wishes and Jewel, but struggled to resolve the question. In her world of quantum exploration, the thought experiment played a role. She performed such an experiment.

I would love to see some fruit trees, she thought.

Ted and Siglinde pressed on as the scientist examined the forest carefully, hoping to see some fruit in response to her thought. Nothing appeared.

Damn, there is no reaction. She thought. *Perhaps, if I say it aloud...*

"Ted," she said, "I am curious that there are no fruit trees anywhere. I would think apple and pear trees at least would be something the Oshki would enjoy."

Less than 100 meters further, they came onto an apple tree with ripe fruit.

Pater appeared.

"Thank you for the apple tree," Siglinde said.

"Come with me," Pater glanced at the fruit tree, ignored Siglinde's words, and ambled into the forest. Pater did not control what Jewel might do. He knew that Siglinde's thoughts lay open to him and Jewel, but if she believed she had to verbalize, it would hide that fact. They calculated that if Siglinde knew she could keep no secrets, it might cause a mental breakdown. They wanted the opposite, a mental strengthening of this intriguing human scientist.

Siglinde followed Pater; her hand clutched Ted's as she basked in the apparent success of her experiment.

Now if I only understood how and why, she thought. *Is Ted involved? Pater knows.*

I'm not doing it. Ted returned the thought. *What is Pater up to? The how is obvious, simple quantum processes, but the why is the real question. This all drives me and my people crazy. We thought we understood the galaxy. After Earth, Jewel is our biggest concern. We dislike not knowing.*

Walking behind their guide, they could not see Pater's smile.

Siglinde did not think the mystery of Jewel hid dark horror. She felt safe with Ted, but more so, she felt benevolence from Jewel and its inhabitants, including her prime suspect, Pater. Whatever the secret of Jewel might be, it did not threaten, but frustrated. Still, requiring the verbal request puzzled Siglinde. She was sure that the night they had arrived, her thoughts alone triggered some change in the environment. It seemed like the fuzzy data that she had often seen in her work. As with that, it would require more experiment to resolve the uncertainty. She loved reproducible results, but Jewel teased.

"I still would love to know why you have remained on Jewel when you could have easily reached the stars." Siglinde said.

Pater paused and fixed his dark eyes on Siglinde.

"But the stars come to us," Pater said.

A crystal hanging from Pater's neck flashed in the sun.

Where have I seen one of those jewels before? Siglinde wondered.

Ellie, love, Ted thought. *She and RoH have crystals much like this one.*

Ted could have said it aloud, but Pater read his thoughts and smiled.

I'm smelling a rat, Siglinde thought back. *I'm not sure if it's real, but it's making my brain feel funny, and I feel like I did in first year university when I absorbed so much new stuff. It felt and feels like my brain grew, or at least changed.*

Pater's smile deepened.

The short path led to a small collection of shelters. The structures did not remind Siglinde of a tropic island, but were more like stemless mushrooms that reflected the subdued sun of the woods. Immense trees resembling Earth's conifers soared high above. Soft needles carpeted the ground. A central circle of benches sat in the clearing. An older woman, dressed in a loose, grey coverall similar to Pater, waited with several Oshki on a long, curved bench. A jewel hung from her neck.

"Mater," Pater kissed the woman on the top of her head and sat beside her. Siglinde sat to the woman's left and Ted sat between his love and an Oshki.

Mater's thoughtful gaze penetrated Siglinde's eyes as if she stared into her soul.

"You are of Nova Species Human," Mater said, "and one of the best of them. You are, as communication suggested."

"What communication?" Siglinde asked.

"We expected your visit," Mater said. She did not elaborate that RoH's evaluation of Siglinde in her grandfather, Charlie Keys' kitchen, had spread via the Specie 2's fleet.

Ted smiled. Siglinde blushed. Mater had explored Ted's feelings and his connection to Siglinde and discovered it went beyond the physical. Ted loved Siglinde and her mind. Even though she knew the story of Ellie and RoH, Mater found it a pleasing curiosity that a Species 2 entity felt human love.

Mater knew that would deepen because of their stay on Jewel. It was part of the hope.

"You are interesting," Mater said

"Siglinde, you and your friend Liz are the first modern humans to be brought here. The intellectual progress by humans in the past thousand years impresses us."

Mater knew her statement was not completely true, but the issue had no importance. The word modern would reduce the deception and plant the seed for Siglinde to understand the truth of Jewel.

"You all look human," Siglinde said. "Why did you mention one thousand years?"

"So it is," Pater intervened, "but the laws of physics dictate our morphology, DNA, as is yours."

Siglinde frowned, and still sought to know what a thousand years might mean.

"On Earth, we thought we understood that high functioning sentient beings did not need to look like Earthly bi-pedal primates." Siglinde said. "There are those who claim DNA may not be the basis for all life."

"So far," Mater said, "DNA is the only mechanism in the galaxy for reproduction in living things. Soon, we hope to discover if that applies in other galaxies, at least one other galaxy."

"From the Andromeda galaxy, the Great Companion," Ted said.

Mater frowned and looked at Pater. This human scientist had become more complex and perceptive than anyone had thought a human might be.

Species 2 knows about the interloper. The revealing might be sooner than we had planned, Pater thought.

It seems so, Mater replied. *Developments with RoH must advance.*

The situation on Earth is maturing. Delay here might not be necessary. Pater concluded.

Anya reports that the Liz human is equally perceptive, Mater thought.

Anya is emotionally attracted to that human, Pater added. *It is both a possibility and a challenge.*

Neither Ted nor Siglinde could hear the exchange.

"So far," Ted said, "our species have found no life that is not DNA based. Shapes and appearance differ, and sentient species can have strange bodies, but the bilateral configuration and ability to manipulate the opposable thumb structure exists in some variant in all technical species, including ours. There are intelligent but non-technical species as well, mostly water dwellers, and some of them lack symmetry. We surmise, but cannot prove, all galactic life has a common origin."

"Ah, the diaspora from the nexus of life," Pater said. He rubbed his beard thoughtfully. "We discuss this idea with the Oshki. We suspect it is true. The physical characteristics of visitors seem to confirm our speculation."

"This mytery keeps the children busy and out of trouble," Mater laughed.

"I would have thought no one ever got into trouble here." Siglinde said.

"No," Pater said, "but everyone creates and sometimes some are playfully annoying. There is a popular fictional distraction, both as written stories and plays under the general genre of the tales of the naughty twins. The little scallions, the protagonists are a male and female and they create much vicarious havoc. It's all great fun."

"They make fun of Pater and me," Mater said. "In the next few decades, I intend to write an episode where we get our revenge. I will exile them to the far-lands."

"What are the far-lands?" Siglinde asked.

"You saw from your ship," Pater said. "Jewel has three major land masses. The other two have populations not unlike us, but who must work for their sustenance. They have no mechanical helpers like we have; as you have at your abode."

"Art," Ted said.

"In my story," Mater said, "those impish twins will join those people in their daily struggles. It will be great fun."

"I would like to see those populations," Siglinde said.

Mater and Pater exchanged glances. Siglinde's learning the complete story of Jewel would complete the plan, and again, events on Earth had sped up the timeline. Still, the time was not yet.

Away from the small group on the bench, a pair of Oshki sat on stone benches at a small stone table. They played a game that resembled Earthly chess with pieces of intricately carved stone. One side shone with a brilliant quartz white. The opposing pieces sparkled with a soft amber colour. Liz's ex-girlfriend geologist would have identified that as Citrine, a variant of pure quartz. Each piece had intricate carving, and yet none were duplicates, as in Earth chess pieces. The players seemed to know the significance of each piece, but Ted, and certainly not Siglinde, could tell from a distance what the ranking of each might be.

The game fascinated Ted. His star travellers had eliminated competition of every type. They had no drive to rise above any other, even in games. Games prevented boredom, but the universe held enough interest that Ted and all of Species 2 had never found boring.

On Earth, in his high school phase that prepared him for his extended service on Earth, Ted had found the sports competitions involving the school teams, the Spartans, to be upsetting. The partisan rivalries had ugliness mixed in with school solidarity. He knew that Ellie and RoH did not seek that kind of conviviality. Team sports seemed to prepare the population to accept war both as players and cheerleaders. RoH had expressed a different opinion to the fleet. Her observations suggested that fanatics for a team meant humans had a great hunger for conviviality and group identity that went beyond the small groups who could function in unity and peace. This encouraged RoH, that this might mean humans could achieve equity and empathy in larger numbers and perhaps the whole global population. It was the goal, and the change would save any advanced human society. Ted wondered how a population of Oshki, mutually caring and united, might allow for competition. That would support RoH's thinking.

Pater noticed Ted's interest in the game. He had followed Ted's thoughts, and Ted's history on Earth fascinated him. It resembled other stories he knew of alien operations on Earth and reminded Pater that Ted's species had a flaw in its make-up. It excited Pater, and all of Species 1 that species 2 had finally recognized that. Of course, it had taken their accidental interaction with the Nova Species Human to create Ellie and to show them. That had happened to the Miigis, Species 1, millennia earlier. Pater saw the connection that both the Miigis and Species 2 had learned of their flaw from humans, and both had taken the same path to restoration of empathy.

"The game is an off-shoot of mathematical training," Pater said. "The actual game is a direct mental dialogue between the players and the table is a way to mark progress. They really seek new permutations and strategies. The winner is the one who finds the most. Lately, meaning in the past many decades, most games have ended in ties. Mathematically, we could not have used every combination, but they become harder to find. I know the carved pieces puzzle you, but each represents a term in some equation. The players define the terms of reference for each piece before they begin, and capture a piece once they express it in a player's mathematics. Each equation must be defendable in terms of logic and convention. Every game is unique. The pieces will represent different factors for each game, depending on what the opponents agree to beforehand. The game you see now is based on some abstract quantum theory. I have been too busy in my mind to tell you which one."

"This pair is actually a bonded couple and likely will go off to celebrate their tie in some intimate way."

"Sex," Ted smiled.

"Likely," Pater agreed. That outcome seemed normal to Pater. "In the end, these games build love and solidarity. Everyone always takes joy in the other's success." Pater turned back to Siglinde. Ted focused on the game.

At the table, each player accumulated a group of captured pieces. The players frowned in concentration.

Ted had playfulness beyond the normal in his species, but being on Earth for a few decades taught him to have fun, at least Ted's idea of fun. Every individual from the collective reported a similar inspiration, although the new workers blamed RoH for their creativeness. Ted could not. His life on Earth had begun ten years before her conception, so he had learned to "lighten up" at Jefferson High School on Earth long before RoH's impishness. Before he had fallen in love with Siglinde, he had thought humans to be a bad influence. Now that he had learned from Ellie and RoH, and basked in Siglinde's unconditional care, he saw things in a more open way. The star travelling diaspora had become as much interested in Ted as any human hybrid. Ted was unaware thar Earth had influenced him as much as Jewel would change Siglinde, but through different processes.

On the board, the captured pieces of each player moved about. The players seemed not to notice, but when one captured a piece; their group suddenly jumped up and down and rattled on the stone surface as if cheering. This mimicked the side line antics that Ted had observed at a Jefferson High School Spartan football game.

The players startled and looked at Ted. They met his human-like grin with smiles.

Species 2 for the win, they both mentally shouted to Ted. All the Oshki, Mater and Pater laughed. All the pieces on the table gyrated wildly, and not because of Ted's mental tricks, but from the players.

We will do this always now, the players thought together. *Go, Spartans, Go.*

Siglinde did not know why they all reacted and focused on her lover, but she startled as she felt an incoherent mental whisper of the exchange. She almost got the unspoken joke. Siglinde felt a change.

That's new, Siglinde thought. She had just experienced a hint that Jewel had expanded her brain using her internal high level of thought. The quantum potential in her lay frustratingly hidden beyond her consciousness.

Active, inquiring minds provided fertile ground for brain growth. Siglinde had begun the journey to be Nova Species Human, Pure Variant Beta. She would need much growth and learning, but Mater and Pater saw the future, if she remained on Jewel for an extended time. On Earth, without the gentle modifications that Jewel could provide, it would take generations for human minds to advance enough. Siglinde would need to remain on Jewel long enough to understand and control her growing ability before returning to Earth. If not, she might do more harm there. They wanted her to remain longer, and now they planned how to inspire her to stay, but they could not force her. A visit to the far lands might be enough.

Mater and Pater had watched the growth process in Oshki newborns, but they had the right genes to start. The divergence between those hybrids on Jewel and the test population left on Earth had revealed the need for Jewel. So far, the genetically pure populations on the other continents had not developed as quickly as the Oshki. The ongoing investigation had yet to reach any definite result. Siglinde's change signalled an entirely new process, and it tested the purpose of Jewel. They originally hoped that the far-land populations would manifest such change, but so far they had observed nothing. Unlike the test population that had remained on Earth a thousand years before, they did not share Oshki genes. They speculated that Siglinde's superior mind, at least superior in its training and use, had made her more susceptible to the physical changes required.

Do you think Ted of Species 2 will manifest changes as well? Pater asked Mater.

The experiment in the Crystal Mountains shows perhaps he will. Mater answered.

I wonder, thought Pater. *They are much closer to the power in the crystals.*

At some point, they would have to reveal all and offer Siglinde the choice of returning then, or extending her stay to step into a much different future. Pater and Mater did not fully understand Siglinde's desire to explore knowledge and the universe. That hunger had driven her into science. Perhaps if they could arrange with Species 2 that

Ted would remain, that would motivate Siglinde. Ted would understand, but the Earth woman had to keep free will. Coercion produced boring and useless results.

Siglinde would be devastated and probably die if Ted left. Mater thought.

Yes, it is so, and I think Ted may stay with her as long as she lives. Pater replied.

The longer she remains here, the longer that will be. Mater answered.

It will be so even after she returns to Earth. Pater thought.

"Why are there differences on those other continents?" Siglinde asked. "I would think humanoids on a planet would have more similarity in culture or at least have evolved similar mental ability."

"We all know of these places. The Oshki understand Jewel's nature, but we normally do not communicate with those others. We also are curious about the answer to your question. As the process on Jewel progresses, we hope to understand that."

It struck Siglinde that Pater's words sounded like a lead investigator discussing an ongoing experiment.

"Is it forbidden to go there?" Ted asked.

"It has not been done," Pater said. "It is a fact, and so it must be. They are not to be influenced."

Siglinde frowned. *If she were here, RoH would say from her love of Earthly slang that she smelled a rat.* As a scientist, Siglinde suspected anything that did not have factual support. She had noticed a sometimes subtle look or hesitation in Pater or Mater's eyes when they said things. Siglinde's feelings that they were not always open with the truth bothered her. She did not detect a threat, but it seemed to mean something.

Why... she wondered.

Once more, Pater looked to Mater.

This Earthling is clever, he thought. *I don't think we want to be the rats here.*

Mater nodded, but both shared a mental chuckle.

Jewel is much like a maze, Mater thought, *but there are many groups experiencing that maze at the same time and in different ways.*

Mater looked at the Oshki in the village.

"So, we wonder about the galactic diaspora," Pater said. He wanted to get the discussion away from Jewel. It was not yet time. The human's curiosity required slow feeding.

"We have analyzed many life forms," Ted said. "Although there are countless unique life forms, some are impossible to believe they could exist. Most planets with life show various stages of what we think of as normal evolution."

"Earth is an example of the diversity of fossils and current life forms." Siglinde said.

"That is why we were so interested in Earth long before the path of Ellie and RoH began." Ted said. "Earth is a living example of what we have found in the fossil history on many worlds that have passed through the Earth phase and withered. Earth is a kind of living museum of galactic life. I doubt the bizarre variety of life forms spread around the part of the galaxy we have visited would shock human scientists. The way humans have destroyed so much of that life saddens us. Earth's treasure really belongs to the galaxy, not only humans."

"That life is everywhere," Pater said. The sureness of his words startled Ted.

"You sound like you know that for sure, but you have never left this planet." Ted said.

Pater and Mater said nothing. The growing suspicions in the minds of Ted and Siglinde marked the expected path of their stay on Jewel. To the people of Jewel, it was not a test of the human or Species 2, but Mater and Pater held the hope they would get an insight into their guest's intelligence. Of course, the Jewelians already understood that both species were intelligent. So far, these two, and the one called Liz, had provided satisfying and encouraging confirmation.

The entity, now self-named RoH, represented a completely different development in galactic evolution and one that exceeded the actuality of Mater and Pater. These old, wise ones felt a surge of humility at any thought of RoH. Her name, revealed her love of her grandparents, cemented her love of Earth, and her existence bound her forever to the galaxy.

They knew that the being, RoH, had a deep love of Earth and would always long for it as home. Optimism lay with her deciding to embrace the galaxy, but they knew, hopefully in a far future, that RoH would return to the Earth she loved because both RoH and the Earth had survived. In the end, they hoped, once RoH realized her essence, that she would satisfy the galactic need before she allowed herself the comfort of home.

Liz, under the conflicted guidance of Anya, was determined to explore. Anya struggled as she tried to combine her personal longings with keeping Liz's quest within the intended time line of the overall strategy, even if Anya did not fully understand that plan. Both Liz and Anya would find their journey frustrating and fulfilling. The pair of women would learn much about themselves and the reality of Jewel.

Mater and Pater found new excitement. After a thousand years, a change had arrived on Jewel.

"Can we visit those other continents?" Siglinde asked.

Siglinde, in her scientific persistence, pulled the conversation back to the thread that Mater and Pater would rather avoid, but they refused to manipulate the humans. To discover how fast a horse could run, one could not hobble the horse.

Chapter 10

Dreams of the Siren Sea

I must go down to the seas again, to the lonely sea and the sky,
  - John Masefield.

Anya held Liz' hand and guided her in a twisted path among the trunks of massive coniferous trees. The pleasing texture of the rough bark reminded Liz of her camping times beneath red pines in the temperate-boreal transition on Earth.

Liz did not feel a breeze, but the forest provided the perfect temperature and humidity. She perspired as she might on Earth, but did not feel discomfort. The land sloped slightly, and they followed a path along that grade and only slightly downward.

I suppose the land should fall towards the sea, Liz thought. *Where is Anya taking me?*

"We are heading to a little village of my friends," Anya said. "It is near the sea. Everyone wants to meet you."

"I hope to meet many," Liz replied.

"Everyone knows all about you, all of what I know, but to meet physically is a higher pleasure. I have been physically separated from the others since you arrived. I look forward to being together."

"Oh, I'm sorry if my being here is a problem."

"You are the opposite of a problem," Anya squeezed Liz's hand. "You are special."

"Of all of my guides when I did fieldwork, you are the best." Liz squeezed back.

"How did you get involved in the hunt for aliens on Earth?" Anya asked.

"I head the sub-team that would interact with aliens if we ever got to talk with them." Liz laughed. "We weren't hunting them. We knew Ted's species existed. My bunch of hot-shots had intended to swoop in and explore alien culture, if they had any. Let's just say that humans are naïve about the galactic community.

"Ellie and her daughter made me obsolete. They are the best for translating star travelling culture into human terms. They recruited their human spokespeople. I'm part of that plan, but I have no clue what I'm supposed to be or do."

"Yes, her daughter RoH, as she calls herself. I can see how she would exceed everything. I'm glad you are dealing with this alien. You are definitely not redundant to me."

Anya tapped her chest and felt a surge of happiness at having met RoH two Earth years before.

The little girl had been polite, but RoH had stared at Anya then.

"You are special," RoH had said. Anya still wondered what "special" might mean. She assumed a special role. Perhaps being with Liz and supporting the human's learning fulfilled that purpose. Anya felt in her heart that she would find more.

"As for your purpose in all this, Liz, I too am ignorant; however, I know you make me happy and that would be enough. Still, you teach me, and maybe one day you will teach humans."

"Anya," Liz said, "you don't seem alien."

"That's because I'm a nice person and I like you."

"True, but I don't just mean you personally, but what appears to be your people, your Oshki. You seem, oh I don't know, human."

"I think that's a consequence of DNA. Pater has been discussing this with Siglinde." Anya said.

Liz eyed Anya.

"What would we find if we did a genetic analysis? She asked.

"Me," Anya said, giggled, and pulled Liz towards a clearing in the forest.

The travellers burst into a meadow where a crowd of expectant Oshki faced them. Liz had seen that look in several African villages as a warm greeting to a stranger. This gathering gave her the same feeling of welcome. What amazed the human scientist was that these people had been expecting them. Liz thought Anya had mentally announced their arrival.

Most of the people were young. Several children, perhaps pre-teenagers, laughed with the others, and soon Liz experienced what seemed like never-ending hugs. Only in Africa, on Earth, had she felt such a greeting. They welcomed her home. Part of her euphoria came from many minds exploring hers and leaving a subconscious memory of care. It felt as if everyone desired to be close to her.

She's mine, came gently but firmly from Anya's mind to the Oshki. Liz could not hear, but while the greetings persisted, they became softer and gentler. The smiles never ceased.

While the happiness did not end Liz's curiosity about all things on Jewel, it reinforced her growing feelings of safety and being home. It mimicked her emotional life on Earth; her estrangement from her family and the reassuring love from others.

Food appeared, and several Oshki sat close while a few gathered and sang. Liz ate, nodded, smiled and tried to keep up with the questions and comments. Liz's dark skin held particular fascination. Every Oshki wanted to touch her and had unlimited questions about Earth. Their deep knowledge of her home planet impressed Liz, but that added to her curiosity.

How do these sophisticated residents of a distant moon-planet know so much about Earth? Why is Earth so important to them? Liz wondered.

During field research, Liz would try to make notes of subtleties in the group such as pairings, family groupings and an obvious social structure. That provided a framework for understanding. Liz discerned no status system here, but saw hints of parings expressed by various Oshki, always being close to a specific other and exchanging subtle expressions and touches. These high mentally powerful beings still sought physical connection.

Liz noticed the children seemed to be in age cohorts. One group neared human puberty, and another was about six years younger. Liz saw no babies.

"Anya," Liz said. "The youngsters seem to be grouped by age."

"Yes," Anya said, "we space reproduction out so that children get full attention for their important formative years, and we make sure that each bunch has a good number of playmates. We decided that four made for a healthy minimum. That is important for their development. In this village, the number of children is six, and the spacing is six years. It is the same in all Oshki villages. The next cohort is in gestation. The population can grow more, but in a few centuries the resources of Jewel will reach their limit, and then the population will stop expanding."

"On Earth, we have a saying that it takes a village to raise a child." Liz smiled towards a group of curious youngsters.

"We do that here," Anya said. "We all have the words Mater or Pater in our names. That is both a remembrance of our lineage, but it is also a reminder that each of us is responsible to each other, and the young. Believe me, children can be a handful, even here."

Anya tapped her foot on the ground and reminded Liz of Jewel.

"The most dangerous time in our lives occurs when we develop our quantum abilities." Anya said. "Children must learn to control that, and it can get wild. Fortunately, it usually happens around puberty as maturity speeds up. Still..."

Anya laughed as her voice trailed off.

"How do you decide who reproduces? Who is to be a parent?" Liz wondered if there were ceremonies and celebrations akin to human rites of passage from child to adult.

"Physical intimacy is a constant. We care for each other, so there are never conflicts. Usually, conception and gestation are in vitro, although a few experience the natural process of pregnancy. The resulting child's given name reflects the parental sperm and zygote donors, but no one possesses a child. They become us, our responsibilities, as soon as they are born. Every new one becomes the 'we' when they reach puberty. There is; however, a ceremony marking the parental genetic connection, and we repeat that at the puberty passage celebration. Children sleep with their actual parents, but that diminishes with age and might end at puberty. The key is to transmit love and empathy to each and, of course, care for the group, the all."

Liz barely hid the excitement. This seemed to be a deliberate enhancement of human tribal culture, but it felt so cold and calculating, as if it were an experiment. She shuddered at the memory of an old Earth story, Brave New World. Liz hoped that Jewel, at least the Oshki, had taken the exact opposite direction from that eugenic dystopia.

"You don't select for certain genes?" Liz asked.

"That is futile," Anya said. "Genetics doesn't work that way, and spontaneous variety strengthens the Oshki. Uniformity would likely mean the end of us."

"Yes, eugenics was an abhorrent travesty on Earth," Liz said. "Will you ever be a mother?"

Liz meant it to be a casual question.

"Oh, yes," Anya said. "I hope to, one day. They say it is special and I love being with the young.

"You know," she eyed Liz with some unease, "that genetic material can come from any gender, whether their natural reproduction is sperm or ovum. We have processes to create a healthy zygote from any two individuals, male or female."

Liz had conflicting images that cycled between a Huxley dystopia and a sunny hillside. She also struggled with the sterile technicality of Anya's statement. That contrasted with her implied meaning for her relationship with Anya, a meaning that perhaps barely existed in Liz's hope. Regardless of their superficial gender, anyone could be a father or a mother.

Liz puzzled over the details while she savoured the distracting interactions of the community and the good food. She did not know how the thought came, but her observations of the hints of parings appeared to be like the relationship she and Anya had developed. When Liz peeked, she caught Anya's copper face full of care as she gazed at Liz. The throng treated the two friends as one such couple.

There's something here I'm not getting, Liz thought. A hopeful solution presented, but it required Liz to be brave, to hope, perhaps too much, too much to touch that answer.

A frustrated Anya gazed at Liz and yearned. She would keep her promise and not pry into Liz's mind, but her desire would never cease.

Several robots delivered food and drink to the group. Liz savoured an offering of strange, but delightful fruit, and a cool sweet drink. Earth development had been standard in the galaxy, and several worlds existed that had verdant flora and where fauna had only reached a simple stage of evolution. These worlds had yielded a strange variety of edible fruits and other vegetable delights. The food factories of Jewel could reproduce these from the genetic codes retrieved from these worlds. Jewel could have given the human tourists Earth varieties, but they shared what the Oshki felt were better delights. Ted and Siglinde were on their honeymoon and Jewel, via the Oshki, had decided that the exotic fit with that celebration. Liz experienced Anya's favourites.

The drinks contained no alcohol or chemicals, but the refreshments deepened Liz's contentment. She enjoyed her status as an honoured guest. Being a scientist could wait.

"No one seems to do any work." Liz said.

"We have no need." Anya said. "The mechanicals and Jewel do the work. Our purpose is to think, and fun helps us do that. Serious thought requires mental relaxation and creative expression like music or painting. The children take part in all we do. Boredom can become hard for the children, so we challenge them early. These have learned much already," Anya pointed to the frolicking children, "and they are perhaps the most creative. Even the gardening is innovative with competition that is both serious and friendly. Physical effort and labour is a good thing, and so gardening adds to that. We never allow mechanicals to work in the gardens, which become places to think and discuss. Our vegetable gardens are just through those trees, on a south facing slope. Everyone wins in the end, at the garden feasts."

"How do you pollinate the flowers?" Liz asked.

"We fertilize by hand," Anya said. "What are you thinking? I don't understand."

Liz decided that explaining the intricacies of the Earth pollination process would take too long, and opened her mind to Anya.

"Read my mind," Liz said. She thought about bee pollination and as many insects as she could.

Anya fixed her with a wide-eyed gaze and then closed her eyes. Anya's smile grew. She learned more than entomology in her brief glimpse into Liz's thoughts; she found more hope than she deserved.

"We never learned that," Anya said, "although Jewel tells me it is all in the data banks. Perhaps Jewel will decide to make those insects. I guess never found it necessary, and so not done. You and Siglinde have already altered Jewel."

"The spin-off might be bee keeping and making delicious honey." Liz said. "Please, let's keep my mind off limits again."

"I hear honey is also a term of endearment, a metaphor for someone loved." Anya said.

"Honey is also sticky," Liz said. "Relationships can become sticky."

Liz watched a machine attendant as it gave attentive service to everyone and tried not to think of metaphorical honey.

"On Earth," Liz said, "they promised us a life like this because of automation." She nodded at the faithful mechanical servant. "That never happened for most."

"Why," Anya asked.

"Our rulers used mechanization to accumulate more wealth and power for themselves. They shared little with the majority. It's the root of Earth's problem now. Ellie made that clear to humans, but so far it has done little good."

Anya frowned. She had followed the reports. RoH and Ellie and Species 2 worked hard to make a change on Earth. They thought they had achieved progress and had more hope than when they first reached Earth. Time, and humans, would tell. Jewel had no such problems.

"That is alien to me," she said. "The idea of accumulating for personal gain is not part of Jewel."

Liz wondered if narrow experience handicapped these mentally powerful residents of Jewel. To a human used to the cut and thrust of Earth cultures, Anya and the others in this village seemed to be naïve. Yet, the Oshki had gentle contentment and lacked for nothing. Most humans struggled for what had constantly been an unreachable goal of personal wealth.

But then, she thought, *perhaps it is humans who suffer the narrowness of experience and imagination. Our self-importance keeps us from a galactic understanding. Those African villagers I met had a happy contentment that reflects the Oshki here. Perhaps humans work harder to survive, but that seems to be the only difference.*

Liz remained ignorant of the freely available energy that allowed Jewel to function as it did. Anya and the

Oshki lacked the same awareness because they had never had to consider it. The residents of this part of Jewel equated to fish that remained unaware of the water that sustained them. They had nothing to compare it.

"Is this," Liz nodded to the merry crowd, "why you never aspired to go to the stars?"

"The stars come to us," Anya said, and she hugged Liz. Anya knew that while Liz struggled to admit her emotions, she welcomed Anya's hug.

The day progressed with fun and frolic. They enjoyed games, songs and dancing. Almost everyone played a variation of drums and wind instruments and took turns providing the music. The Oshki pulled Liz into various dances, and she reluctantly gave in to a cappella karaoke and sang an Earth ballad in approximate tune, but she felt fortunate that no one insisted she take part in an unfamiliar game.

The match seemed to be a game of tag. Liz could not identify any rules, but the competition reminded her of one called "poison tag" that she had played as a youngster. At the beginning, the group quietly stood for some time and Liz thought it strange.

"What's happening?" She asked.

"They are mentally repeating quantum equations to each other. The first person to make a mistake will become the chaser, and the rest will try to escape their touch."

As if on cue, the group suddenly burst into derisive laughter and everyone rushed away from a woman.

"She left out a power sign," Anya said. "I made a mistake earlier, but they left me out because I am your consort."

Liz regarded Anya with puzzlement. Apparently the Oshki regarded Liz and Anya as a bonded couple. Consort seemed to imply a stronger bond than friendship.

The adults ran around the meadow, with the chaser changing several times. Then, as one was about to be tagged, they shot into the air ten metres above the grass. The mob howled.

"They broke the rules," Anya said, "showing off for you, but watch this."

All the locals could levitate and shot about in unflattering poses that highlighted their skimpy dress. The shiny material that Jewel provided caught the sun in a mesmerizing kaleidoscope of colour, light and immodest transparency. The iridescence rose and fell with the shape of the pursuit. Liz felt vertigo and feared for their safety, but no one fell despite skimming the meadow and gyrating wildly. Laughter dominated it all.

"They make themselves fly," Anya said, "but they can also interfere with each other's fields. Now it is really a strange variation of wrestling. Starting the aerial version is a strategic mistake. It's harder to avoid a tag as pursuers can reach you from any direction. Notice how quickly the target changes."

The sight did not surprise Liz. She had seen Ted perform similar gravity defying tricks, although he had not performed such gymnastics. The scene had reached a blur and Liz could not watch, fearing a catastrophe, but none of the frolicking crowd ever collided. Liz had seen flocks of Earth birds behaving in the same way.

I wonder if they are just showing off for me; she thought. *I doubt they have any need to brag to someone they know is mentally inferior, and I doubt conceit is in their nature.*

Liz looked at Anya. *I wonder if Anya can levitate us to the Crystal Mountains.*

Anya did not let Liz see her discomfort at the thought, and she did not respond. Liz trusted her not to peek into her mind, but in her desire, Anya could not resist the occasional snoop.

Stop it, the thought came from Mater.

Yes, mother, Anya giggled.

You long; you lust, but Liz must trust, Mater's thought came with love.

Mater, you are a poet.

Anya giggled aloud, but Liz did not notice.

Anya squeezed Liz' hand.

"While all this play is happening in the physical, everyone you see is involved in a deep discussion of the quantum reality of the universe. We struggle with the energy problem. This thought thread has been going on for centuries. Not even Pater and Mater understand." Anya said.

"Who are Pater and Mater?" Liz asked.

"They are my, in fact for most here, our father and mother. We are their family." Anya answered.

"Even though, to you, this village might appear to be focused on deep thought, that appearance is only partly true. For deeper, more staid contemplation, scientific exploration; you must go to the village of Pater and Mater. The best of us go there, although our connection of minds makes physical proximity unnecessary. Still, we do it for conviviality. They play more subdued games."

"I would love to meet them," Liz said.

"Your friends are with them now. You will meet one day."

Liz put serious thoughts aside and enjoyed the relaxation. As night fell, the gathering dissolved as pairings disappeared into various types of lodge. Anya led Liz to a raised, open platform beneath a rainproof covering. It had no walls but two soft beds. Liz hoped to reach the Crystal Mountains in the morning. As she drifted into sleep, Liz heard waves on a beach. She slumbered to the gentle sound of raindrops and imagined Anya guiding her to the sea. As night fell, beneath the sound of the rain, the swell washed the beach hidden beyond the trees and added a gentle beat to nature's music.

Liz dreamed.

Liz drifted through trees, feet barely feeling the ground and left no prints on the soft forest floor. Dampness surrounded her. Light shone from beyond the trees, where the sound of the sea beckoned. Her body warmed, flushed, feelings of love filled her. She yearned for the sand, the light, the sea.

Dazzling light glinted from beyond the aqua green. Ripples of gentle waves broke the brilliance. Liz longed; she needed, she lusted.

A hand felt hers. She could not turn to look, but she knew... Anya... Anya...

Anya appeared between Liz and the sea; she smiled; Anya retreated slowly to the water and never taking her gaze from Liz.

Faster, Liz cried. I must go. We must go. The crystals, the crystals...

Anya backed into the water, opened her arms.

Come, Liz, come to me...

Liz longed to rush into the sea, towards the Crystal Mountains, into Anya's arms, but heavy legs betrayed her. Still her feet left no prints, but she struggled through air that now felt heavy, a viscous liquid. Liz needed; she longed for; she must reach the mountains and her love. The Crystal Mountains beckoned in brilliant flashes of reds and blues and yellows, hiding, promising...what?

They retreated, no matter how far she walked. Liz stumbled, fell, Anya lifted her from the sand and they floated towards the water, towards the siren sea and the mysterious crystal peaks.

Chapter 11

Time travellers, sort of

Time and tide wait for no man.
- Geoffrey Chaucer

Pater had arrived at the cottage just as Ted and Siglinde finished breakfast. A robot escorted the pair home after Pater had warned them to be ready for today.

"Ted," Pater said, "we have asked your ship to carry us. It will get us to the first continent faster than on the surface."

At the edge of the welcoming space, restored to a meadow for Siglinde's benefit, a typical shaft of purple light lifted them into the Species 2 ship. To Siglinde, it seemed in an instant they descended onto the surface of one of the far-lands. The speed at which Pater had acted on their desire to explore mystified both Ted and Siglinde. She thought Pater seemed to have a new urgency. Had something changed?

"Yes," Pater said in reply to her thoughts. "Events in the galaxy and on Earth have changed things."

"How...why," Siglinde asked, but Pater said no more.

This did not reassure Siglinde, but she had long since resigned her fate to events beyond her control.

The ship had set them down at the edge of a crop of grain. A treed windrow separated them from another field, and a cluster of buildings, surrounded by trees, sat about 500 meters on the far side of the field. The vista imitated a centuries old painting of an Earth farm.

Pater eased along the edge of the crop and followed a windrow and a living hedge-fence. The grain had not yet ripened and green ripples danced in the breeze. That same wind carried a pungent, earthy odour of freshly plowed soil that did not exist in the land of the Oshki. The sounds of a farmhand guiding horses and the clink of harness rode the breeze from behind the windrow.

"Pater, this place looks and smells different from your home," Siglinde said.

"Yes, this continent, and the third we will visit, differ from ours. It is necessary for both cropping and hunting, which we Oshki do not need to do.

"We don't want to harm any part of this. It's their major food source." Pater said. He swept a hand over the rippling grain. "They do not have our industrial food sources."

The rustic scene reminded Siglinde of Earth, and Ted, who had spent most of his life on a ship, felt exhilaration. This vista contrasted with the enclosed, park-like comfort of the forest on the Oshki continent. It seemed natural.

This feels more like home, Siglinde thought. Her sigh conveyed both her contentment and the minor homesickness of the traveller.

Pater felt Siglinde's emotions. Jewel had not finished with the Earth scientist, but Pater knew that when she eventually returned home, her new insight and love of home would play a large part in the success of the human species, if survival of high order life on Earth became the outcome.

"We will remain invisible to the folks here and observe. If you wish to talk to these people," Pater looked at Siglinde, "then we can consider it. We never intervene in their lives, so I would not desire it, but we will see. They know nothing of us or of the other continents of Jewel."

"We have a joke in the lab," Siglinde said. "Never stick your finger into the experiment."

She suspects, Pater thought. *Mater, I think we must decide.*

Events compel us, my dear. Mater's reply felt happy.

Liz is about to enter the crystals and then she will know.

On Earth, RoH visited the focus of the Earthbound Oshki, and she suspects. She has examined her genetic make-up, and we are certain she is certain. A ship has left for Earth and will offer her future to her. We have no way of predicting if she will accept.

When we conceived RoH, we did not understand where she would take us. There are things beyond the understanding of even the Miigis. Hope lives.

Yes, my Mater, Pater thought in return, *yes.*

The trio strode into a rude barnyard. Animal odours dominated a muddy paddock that lay before unsophisticated, functional, well-built, but old buildings. The larger structures formed an outer ring around the community, a reasonable distance away from a combination of houses and shops that circled a central, dusty inner plaza.

"This is typical for this part of the continent," Pater said. "There are many settlements like this."

The resemblance to an Earth village stunned Siglinde. They had laid it out in the efficient way of villages on Earth, before cheap fossil fuels allowed sub-urban sprawl.

She pondered the livestock in open paddocks and pens. Chickens ranged in the open.

"The animals are Earth domesticated animals: cattle, chickens, sheep, and goats. How is this possible?" Siglinde asked.

Pater considered whether to reveal the truth of these people or postpone it. He delayed. He felt privileged to watch Siglinde's unfettered mind gather and store information and questions. In a life of planned deliberation and galaxy scale mental unity, he had never had the privilege of watching the discovery of the new by a brilliant mind that had not yet united with a larger, cognitive whole. Pater warmed with the thought that once Siglinde had found the mental connections, she would become so much more. This human scientist seemed to be the summation of their original confidence that the human genetic assembly held galactic importance, even in its undiluted form. Species 2 had realized that with Ellie, and now RoH confirmed the ultimate prize. The dispersing of that human emotional overlay of empathy and togetherness promised power beyond the Miigis. It would be the power to understand, not possess. Pater could barely contain this unfamiliar excitement.

Mater, I have this strange emotion in my heart. I never believed I could feel this.

It is a feeling of wonder and exhilaration, Mater replied. *I share it. We are privileged to be here at the nexus of the future. It is a time of wondrous serendipity.*

"It is curious," Pater agreed, but he left Siglinde's question unanswered.

Chickens and small animals wandered about. A goat trotted up and stared.

"I think it sees us," Siglinde said.

"Yes," Pater said, "I have screened us from the residents, but the animals are aware of us. It might keep a horse or cow from knocking us down."

Siglinde reached out and scratched the nanny goat behind an ear. The animal looked contented and pressed against her hand. Siglinde felt a brief rush of homesickness, and her smile betrayed her happiness with the animal. People had petted the goat before and considering the children wandering about, that did not come as a surprise. Kid goats frolicked in the yard under the amused gaze of their nannies.

Siglinde had never lived on an Earth farm and so had no experience with these creatures. The impish goats reminded her of RoH, and Siglinde had the thought that once RoH discovered these rascals, they would be her favourite companions. RoH, goat, and imp all seemed to fit Siglinde's loving image of RoH.

"Let's move on," Pater said.

They reached the square and entered an open-air pavilion that protected various breads and a variety of sweets. People entered with baskets, chose some delights and left. Similar structures purveyed various staple foods.

The people resembled white Europeans. In contrast to anywhere on present day Earth, Siglinde saw no other races. The Earth that Siglinde knew had few places left where various races and nationalities did not mix. Here, she saw a homogeneity that she thought to be artificial and perhaps intentional. Liz would say it looked like Europe before colonialism.

It isn't only the manure that smells here, Siglinde thought. *What is the meaning of this place?*

Pater regarded her with a wide-eyed admiration.

She is intelligent, curious and not easily convinced or influenced. We are right in thinking she is a good fit for her purpose when she returns to her planet. Pater smiled, but kept his thoughts silent.

"They used no money," Siglinde said.

"So I see," Pater said. "In our community, abundance makes everything freely available. It seems this village developed a similar way to distribute needs, but based on labour and cooperation, not done by mechanical slaves."

"This is not commercial activity," Siglinde said. "They simply exchange. No one is recording any transaction. How do they track the balances?"

"They work to produce their needs and luxuries," Pater said. "Their most precious thing is their time. They work to be happy. For these people, enough is all they need and no more. The ledger balance is in the benefit of the entire village, not simply between residents. A monetary ledger is only necessary if someone wants to steal."

"Don't they have bigger obligations, like taxes? Don't they have a government?" Ted asked. While Species 2 had nothing like that, he wondered why a human like culture would not.

"Each village is autonomous," Pater said. "They are small enough to decide among themselves. There are many nearby villages. Occasionally, they meet for discussions, although those times include celebration and fun.

"There is some differentiation in the focus of a village. You notice metal implements and woven cloth. Those come from other villages. This one produces food and shares. Roads are the only common and jointly maintained infrastructure."

Pater pondered the situation. The original intent had been to see if these humans would develop mentally towards higher brain function because of Jewel. He observed an unexpected result. The humans had simply developed an egalitarian culture. He had a hopeful inspiration.

"Siglinde," Pater said, "is this not what Ellie has advocated on Earth?"

"Yes," Siglinde said, "oh, it would thrill her if we did this back home. I'm struck because everyone seems happy. I notice tired faces, but none without some pleasantness. RoH once told me that this results from mutual empathy and care. The purpose of the baker seems to be to fill other's needs. No doubt there is a complex underlay of reciprocation and we would need to take part to understand it. On Earth, we have hidden that deep relationship and connection by using money. Ellie has a hard job trying to convince modern humans into that system of mutual aid, empathy and equity."

Siglinde again felt a flash of homesickness, but suddenly, the 21 light years to Earth no longer seemed important. She did not know how events had progressed on Earth, but a deep confidence that Ellie would prevail washed over her.

All will be well ...

Siglinde was certain. If she talked to Ellie at that moment, she would find much less confidence.

Doing this with nine billion humans is likely impossible. She thought.

"Perhaps," Pater said. "If humans learned to live with just enough, they would find contentment and, likely, the stars."

"If..." Siglinde said.

"We did it," Ted said about Species 2.

They watched transactions in a butcher shop, a tailor, cobbler and a greengrocer. They saw no hint of anything manufactured industrially, although the prevalence of metal tools reinforced Pater's information that somewhere, people made metal goods.

A horse-drawn wagon bearing tools and other hardware circled into the square. They watched an exchange of bags of grain, a few live animals and other food for some wares. The wagon made to leave.

"Let's ride along," Pater said and climbed unseen onto the wagon, making room amongst the few animals and ending up with a chicken in his lap. He laughed as Ted and Siglinde found places on grain sacks. No human saw them.

We saw no sigh of minerals on the other continent, Siglinde thought. *Is this continent different?*

Pater considered enlightening the human, but the time had not arrived. He touched the crystal hanging from his neck.

It will be soon, Pater thought.

As the wagon travelled, Siglinde saw land and dirt different from the Oshki's continent. Rock hills showed definite signs of mineralization. They passed through a valley where deposits of deep red suggested iron hematite. Such places still existed on Earth in places like the Lake Superior region of North America and the weathered plains of Western Australia. Here, their appearance contrasted the quartz bedrock of the Oshki continent.

The wagon paused near a swamp where two men waited. They hefted heavy leather bags onto the rear of the vehicle and forced Siglinde to stand out of the way. The bags contained bog iron, perhaps originating from erosion of the hematite bedrock and bacteria.

Bacteria, Siglinde thought and startled. The Oshki continent seemed sterile as an operating theatre, and here she saw organic chaos similar to Earth.

The men took a chicken and a bag of flour from the wagon and disappeared towards the marsh of a river's mouth. Siglinde looked past to where the river entered the sea.

"If there are tides here, this must be high tide. The water is almost touching the trees." Siglinde frowned. "I would think with the massive mother planet, tides on Jewel should be huge."

Ted shrugged. "We have observed no tides from space," he said.

"That defies all we know about planetary science." Siglinde said. "This planet is strange: weird magnetic fields, pure quartz bedrock, an almost at least in on continent, perfectly smooth gravity and no tides."

Pater observed the pair and felt Siglinde's growing unease. His fascination with the human kept pace with his feeling of a deepening urgency to satisfy her curiosity.

Soon, he thought. Pater looked to the hills as if seeking answers or comfort from Jewel.

The end of the valley answered Siglinde's questions. Smoke and fumes replaced the pristine air of the farm village. While it seemed to be as oppressive as the worst parts of Earth, everything was on a small scale. The pollution came from small forges and simple furnaces that could not have high capacities. Wagon loads of cut wood provided the energy for the smelters and the forges.

Perhaps that's enough, she thought. *If that first farming village is typical, they would only need a few kilograms of metal products a year. I wonder how many other villages exist on this continent.*

Pater found the scenes of human industry, even on these small scales, interesting. The robotic equivalents of the Oshki lay hidden within Jewel and did not use such primitive energy transformations. Only necessary pristine products appeared on the surface.

They only make just enough, Pater thought. *In some ways, these humans have developed a low-tech version of Oshki's existence. These are exciting results and an encouragement for Earth.*

Of course, this continent comprised natural material that was common on most rocky planets in the known galaxy. It allowed the residents to explore, invent and develop technology at an unforced pace.

"This is 18th century Earth technology," Siglinde said. "It is a contrast to your robots."

"We developed differently," Pater said to explain while saying nothing. He offered no more, but he felt excited at this human success.

"How many people live here?" Siglinde asked.

"Population densities are low and perhaps only a few thousand live on the entire continent and spread out so that they don't interfere with each other. About one hundred villages of various purposes share this part and this general social structure. There are hundreds, if not thousands, of your Earth kilometres between different cultures. You soon will see that."

"Populations are controlled naturally, and there is grief here that the Oshki do not share. Medicine is primitive and many females and infants die for reasons linked to birth. That keeps the numbers from exceeding the carrying capacity of the land."

"That seems cruel," Siglinde said. "Can you not intervene?"

Pater frowned, but he did not reply. While he and Mater had no moral problem with the situation, it still unsettled them. They had replaced natural processes long ago with sentient artificial structure and life. They had designed this part of Jewel to explore the differences and to understand how Earth might thrive in natural conditions with some variable parameters. He and Mater had not been part of that work, but they understood it all.

"Like the other village, no one seems to be in any hurry," Siglinde said. "They only rush during certain foundry operations."

"Like the other places, they only work to be happy. They want no profit," Pater said, "but they seek only a balance and enough. When they trade for food, the worth of their labours is only the amount of food required. This is a modified farm village that still grows most of its food. It applies to other communities that specialize, like cloth making, but it is all in balance. It has evolved for one thousand years. The only surpluses they create are to guard against lean times in the fields."

"On Earth, surpluses led to intellectual growth, astronomy and science." Siglinde said.

"And war," Ted added.

"Top down power structures cause war," Pater said. "If those had not developed, perhaps peaceful intellectualism would have led humans to the stars long ago."

"Space travel requires complex industry that is far beyond tribal ability." Siglinde said.

"Or it requires quantum ability," Ted said. "Quantum capability might develop independent of industry."

"Could that happen here?" Siglinde asked.

"Maybe," Pater said. He looked away, unable to hold Siglinde's sight. She had asked a question that had not been part of Jewel's original purpose.

Perhaps, he thought, but left the idea unfinished.

"You mentioned other cultures on this continent," Ted said.

"I sense you have seen enough here," Pater said. "Come with me. I will call your ship."

Pater led them out of sight. While the residents could not see them, they would notice the disturbance of the ship lifting them up. The event became the focus of much discussion amongst the villagers. Several young people gazed at the mysterious flash in the sky and wondered about the stars.

Chapter 12

To the Crystal Mountains

"Alice had begun to think that very few things indeed were really impossible."
-The Adventures of Alice in Wonderland.

Morning light eased in with the lingering, sweet smell of the overnight rain. Liz stirred, rested despite her unsatisfying dream and restless because of it. A robot had expected Liz's awakening and arrived with juice and a coffee. Liz sat on the side of her bed and enjoyed both. She noticed Anya laying in her bed, watching.

Anya tried to sort out her thoughts. *No, my feelings,* she thought. Life on Jewel had satisfied in all of her memory. The mental challenges gave completeness to her life, but now, this human had upset that. Humans represented something else, perhaps an opportunity, maybe to actually visit Earth. Her deep memory, something from the misty past of the Oshki, told her there was more, something cultural. Anya could not yet know what those misty, archetype memories hid. Liz' presence deepened her longing.

"I always enjoy the quiet of the morning," Anya said.

"I don't find the days here demanding." Liz sipped.

"I hope today is more than that," Anya said. "Today, we will go to the sea. Still, I hope we have no stress."

They walked the short way to the beach. Anya hurried ahead, and Liz emerged from the trees. Anya stood on the white sand and walked backwards. She extended her hands towards Liz and drew her to the water. Gentle rivulets gurgled against the shore and raised white foam on the sand as they massaged their feet in the warmth of the Jewelian sea.

The froth reassured Liz that the water, while pristine, must contain organics. It suggested some material washed in from the land and might show that plants and critters lived beneath the waves. She hoped for more wonders from the calm, alluring sea. The surprise would be more exciting than Liz could imagine.

They stood, arm in arm, bare feet rested in the warmth of the gentle surf, and they gazed out to sea. Liz shaded her eyes and saw the tips of the jagged peaks breaking the luminous horizon where the aqua sea melded to the cobalt sky. The arch of the mother planet spanned the sky beyond the peaks and drew a magnificent tapestry of wonder.

The peaceful wash of waves accompanied distant bird calls. Liz wanted the moment to last forever.

"Good morning," came from behind, with the shuffle of feet on the sand. "I wanted to see you off."

Mater approached, and her smile warmed.

"Mater," Anya said, "I'm so glad you approve."

"We approve of it all." Mater looked at the women, and then at the sea. Her eyes found the crystal spires on the horizon and she felt contentment. The women would discover surprises there, but to Mater, the Crystal Mountains meant much more. No part of the original plan called for this day, these two, this Earthling, but also the efforts of Species 2 and the existence of RoH had sped up it all. Mater's heart held a mixture of sadness and excitement.

I have one more job to do. Mater looked at Anya and Liz. *These two must learn and feel love.*

"Liz," Mater said, "you will find answers and mystery there."

She nodded over the water. Mater fell silent as the waves talked and sea-birds squawked, and then said,

"The time approaches when Jewel will reveal all. All must be united, Species 1, Species 2 and the nova humans. Liz," Mater turned to the human scientist, "the purpose of your visit to Jewel will become clear. Do not fear."

If nothing else, Liz felt safe on Jewel. She did not know what Mater meant when she alluded to danger, but Liz prepared to accept whatever the matriarch had in mind.

"Anya, this too is your last lesson. The purpose and truth of the Oshki, of you, lies there. You both will be bound to fulfil destiny, not on the scale of RoH, the seed of new life, but you will draw strength into the galaxy in your own right. You will draw strength and understanding from each other. There is much in nova species human that we wish to spread."

Mater startled both women. Liz felt portent and purpose. She hoped it did not mean suffering. Anya had thought her existence to be complete. Mater suggested that she had only been training and that her learning would complete into a grand purpose.

Liz and Anya trembled.

"Liz," Mater took her hand, "you, Siglinde and many more are the key. Species 2 recognized strength and courage in some humans. We must not lose that, and you must help, and Anya, too."

Mater placed a hand on Liz's and Anya's shoulders. "It binds you both."

Mater smiled and kissed each woman on a cheek. It all reminded Liz of the marriage ceremonies she had witnessed in Africa. Mater talked in riddles and Liz struggled to understand.

"Go now," Mater pointed to an out-rigged canoe that bobbed at the shore. "Travel slowly; there is no rush, and find your answers and yourselves."

Liz and Anya looked at each other. They shared a common, unstated longing that their uncertainties hid. Mater had offered both confusion and hope.

Mater embraced them and then turned abruptly towards the forest. Her mind touched Pater, who wandered on the far side of the planet. The hope for their thousand year journey now lay in sight. Jewel would forever remain their home, but it promised to be a more wonderful place. Mater disappeared into the trees. She prepared to play a cross between

Cupid and an angry Neptune. Mater relished the privilege. Crisis and challenge always led to change. That was something that, until the humans arrived, the Oshki had never felt.

"I have never used one of these boats," Anya said. "It would be easier for me to fly us there."

"And miss the fun?" Liz laughed. "I paddled on a lot of field-work. This looks like a nice little boat, and there won't be rapids or rough water."

Liz pushed the craft off the sand and helped Anya into the bow. She claimed the rear place with a broad paddle and gently pushed away from shore.

"Take that paddle like this and make gentle strokes," she told Anya. "The water is smooth. Twist the paddle into the water so that the force balances to left and right. Don't try too hard and we will be fine."

In a half hour, Anya found a comfortable stroke and mimicked Liz's effort. They sped towards the Crystal Mountains. The gurgle of water along the hulls massaged Liz into a happy torpor. A following breeze eased their efforts. A sail would have helped, but perhaps that was too much to hope for.

Strange, Liz thought. *The warming land should make for an on-shore wind, but this off-shore breeze is perfect. Jewel indeed has surprises, but why is everything so damned perfect?*

Liz embraced the gentleness and the nearness of Anya. She watched the back of her friend's head. Long black hair hung down and rippled in the breeze. The bright horizon silhouetted Anya. Liz had never seen such a comforting sight. While the mountains drew closer, the distance to Anya would not change. Liz thought of the trick of dangling a carrot in front of a donkey to motivate it to move forward. She felt the metaphor applied to her in the boat. This carrot would be so nice.

After a few hours, they rested. A large container sat on the boat's bottom, and they took water and food. Liz rested her hand on her paddle that lay across the gunnels, wondered at the convenient presence of the boat and provisions, and smiled at Anya, who had turned around for lunch. Their eyes met, and both knew, but somehow each felt shyness, as if fearing to break the moment, fearful of the truth and the risk of discovering it.

The owl and the pussycat went to sea,

"Let's get going," Liz finally said, struggling against the emotion that felt too powerful. "I think it's less than an hour."

The crystal peaks loomed in the near distance. The shore lay only a kilometre away.

How can I make it happen? Anya thought.

Leave it to me, Mater's thought reached Anya.

What, Anya thought?

Liz easily paddled. The water rolled from her paddle and slipped astern in diminishing vortexes that disturbed receding bubbles of foam. The warmth and gentleness of the sea lulled. Liz's eyes drooped. She mechanically stroked and drifted into a dream state between wakefulness and comfort.

The owl and the pussycat
Went to sea
In a beautiful pea-green boat

She flowed into a happy place and recited the silly poem.

It hit with no warning. The sea roared with anger. Waves rose from nowhere, wild and mean, as if some monster wanted to torment and kill.

The boat leapt skyward and jarred Liz to alertness. Ugly waves swirled and rose and fell in a vicious attack. The craft twisted and turned in a maelstrom of chaos that threatened to snatch her dream of the Crystal Mountains and take her life. They flung skywards and crashed into a trough of despair, where dark walls of water framed a small bit of blue sky. Tops blew off the waves and soaked the women. The world had gone mad.

Liz screamed. The craft pitched wildly and flew skyward once more. She watched, dumbfounded, as Anya soared high as the violent waves flung the frightened woman into the sea. Her flailing body hit hard and waves hid her.

"No..." Liz screamed.

Water did not scare Liz. She had attended university on a water-polo scholarship. She had never had to deal with such a murderous maelstrom, although her geology student lover had once taken her white-water rafting. They had pitched into rapids, but that had been a short-lived scare that ended in the hands of a powerful guide. This water wanted to kill.

Anya had disappeared. Fear gripped Liz. Her life did not matter. She must save Anya.

"Anya," she cried, "Anya,"

A wave pitched Liz backwards into the surging sea, and she felt the bump of soft flesh. Anya floated unconsciously. The blood on her head marked where her paddle had hit.

Liz grabbed Anya's shirt and hugged her tight. Her free arm dug into the water. The waves threw her backwards as if her efforts did not matter.

"We will not die," Liz screamed. "We will not die."

Her voice struggled to convince her mind that all would be good. The water wanted to kill them. In a brief thought, she wondered if Jewel wanted to keep them from the Crystal Mountains. Liz could not know the reality of the cause, or the measured effect of the waves.

Why could Anya's ability not have saved us? She asked.

Liz stroked and believed they had made progress. Her arm ached. Her lungs demanded air. Liz tried to avoid breathing water.

Liz had closed the gap towards the far shore. The ferocity of the waves declined, and Liz swam with her burden through the crashing surf. The waves now washed her towards that shore and no longer wanted to kill. Liz's legs struggled against the backwash as the beach lay desperately close. An enormous wave surged under them and flung the pair onto the wet sand. Strangely, after that last violence, the water calmed.

What the hell? She asked.

Liz lay, exhausted, with small waves washing her legs, but gladly not drawing her back to the sea. Anya's weight pinned one arm beneath. The inert body demanded action.

"Anya," Liz cried, "Anya..."

The woman did not reply.

Liz pulled her arm from beneath her friend and dragged Anya safely away from the diminishing surf. She felt for a pulse.

Nothing...and no sign of breathing

Liz had to move fast.

Chapter 13

Tribe and tribulation

"We are what we imagine. Our very existence comprises our imagination of ourselves. Our best destiny is to imagine, at least, completely, who and what, and that we are. The greatest tragedy that can befall us is to go unimagined."
*- **N. Scott Momaday***

Pater, Ted and Siglinde stood on a grassy hill on the opposite side of the second continent, far from the agricultural villages. A cordillera of impassable mountains and a wide, parched desolation separated the two places. Siglinde had seen none of this wilderness that contrasted Jewel's normal benevolence. Their brief hop across the continent on the Species 2 star ship had not allowed sightseeing.

The soft meadow they shared with goats and sheep swept down to a hand-cut clearing in the dense forest. When they appeared, the sheep fled to the far corner of the field, but the goats trotted over to investigate. A village of simple huts made of poles and animal hides occupied the clearing, and smoke from cooking fires wafted away on a gentle breeze. Women and children scurried about the community.

"This is a more primitive place," Pater said. "These people have maintained a simple existence of small agriculture, herding, hunting and gathering for many generations. It has stability."

"Except for the goats and sheep, the place looks like a traditional North American native community." Siglinde said. "Why is it that this village and the last place all seem like transplanted Earth cultures?"

"Just so," Pater said. He ignored the question. "We have observed a profound permanence and happiness here. Unlike Earth, at least what we know of Earth, Jewel provides a constant bounty of food and a less extreme climate. This society is not stressed, although it is not without hardship and danger. It has more primitive technology than the previous places had."

"Just like Earth," Siglinde said, "but it is not like you, Oshki. You suffer no want, no struggle, and no danger."

"It is the way we try to live in the galaxy," Ted said. "We employ a profound equality and equity, based on our ability to link our minds and to consider the all. Of course, there is nowhere in the galaxy without danger. Is it similar here?"

"We will enter and observe," Pater said. "If I may, though, it is Species 2's ability to provide unlimited energy that allows your equity and it has reduced the dangers you face. You have eliminated resource shortages and thus the need to fight amongst yourselves. Here, distance and bounty prevent conflict, both externally and internally, and although Jewel provides abundance, here it is realized through work. With the Oshki, mechanicals carry out that work. Again, here they work for happiness and make no surplus except for what might be prudent for a lean harvest or reduced hunting success."

"Sharing in equity would help humans on Earth," Siglinde said. "That is what Ellie and RoH aspire to have there."

"Earth is a place of extremes and struggle," Pater said. "Life on Earth requires more energy and ways to conserve it. Jewel does not demand that of the Oshki. This is more like Earth. This place and the one we just left question how much technology you might want. If one never had the technology, they would not miss having it. Modern Earthlings have frivolous technology and doing without would seem like a collapse. What we see on Jewel does not mimic the predicament on Earth."

"You say Jewel as if it is a live entity." Siglinde said.

Pater said nothing, but eyed the human scientist. He waited for her to make the breakthrough. He constantly monitored her thoughts. She struggled with the implications of the quantum universe that RoH had hinted at when they first met in Charlie Keys' kitchen. She thought of the sentient characteristics of Ted's starship and how that might relate to the planet, Jewel.

Pater knew it was a matter of time before Siglinde resolved the first piece of the quantum puzzle of universal energy relationships. She must not reach that point until humans had learned to get along and live for enough. Otherwise, unlimited energy would be disastrous. They had observed several failed planets that had had fossil energy like Earth had: oil and coal. None had survived that gift of millions of years of stored star energy. Earth followed that trajectory to destruction.

Pater resolved to discuss that more with Siglinde. He knew Ted already understood the energy danger; the risk that without energy and resource restrictions, humans would join the other failed ones by frying the Earth. At least fossil energy was already declining on Earth. They had to find wisdom and empathy first.

RoH, in her incomplete knowledge, had only teased the truth to Siglinde. Ted refused to expedite Siglinde's development. If humans took the step, it would have to come from their grasping of the quantum universe. Siglinde did not yet know that her foot had already risen to make that step. Pater hoped Siglinde would make that breakthrough on Jewel and return to Earth to lead what would be an energy revolution, and combined with Ellie's path to empathy and equity, liberate humanity. Jewel could make that happen. It all depended on Siglinde. Her brain had already begun the journey. Still, humans on Earth had to reach that state of equity and empathy. If they did not, Siglinde had to find the wisdom to avoid leading humanity into a quantum disaster.

"Let's look," Siglinde stepped down the hill.

The laughter of children reached them. The visitors remained invisible to the villagers, so the laughter did not greet them but reflected the happy everyday village life. In an echo of the previous agricultural society, dwellings ringed the centre where a cooking fire burnt low. A roofed pavilion shaded women preparing food and chatting. The children scurried about in play; however, some gathered fuel for the fire and others carried eggs and other raw food to the women. They saw no sign of specialized shops as in the previous village.

The people had copper faces similar to the Oshki. If these people stood beside an Oshki, and dressed in Oshki jumpsuits, Siglinde could not have seen a difference. This contrasted a little with the white in the agricultural community, especially in skin colour.

"Where are the men?" Siglinde asked.

The large animal carcass on a spit over the fire hinted at the answer.

"They hunt," Pater said and pointed to the roasting meat. A child, a pre-teen Siglinde estimated, rotated the roast and occasionally basted it with fat-rendering captured in a large wooden spoon beneath the meat.

"Don't you find that upsetting compared to the way the Oshki receive food?" Siglinde asked.

"Life in the universe is a symbiotic arrangement of one species providing sustenance to another," Pater said. "Sentient beings can reduce the cruelty involved between predator and prey, but it is part of the unity of life. Perhaps other species cannot consider the suffering of the kill, but humans and the rest of us can. It is disheartening that some humans relish in the suffering, but we think that is a cultural artefact based on your greedy cultures, ignorance and inherited mysticism. Humans, left to their nature, do not do that. They kill in need, but honour the sacrifice of their prey."

He nodded towards the villagers and hesitated. Pater seldom made mistakes, but he felt he had erred. He hoped Siglinde did not connect his gesture to his mentioning humans in their natural ways. Pater resolved to be more careful. He knew Siglinde represented a pinnacle of human intelligence and curiosity, and she had already suspected the deception. Liz, with her training, would have understood immediately.

Pater and Mater knew it all. They were the only beings on Jewel, other than the one who dwelt in the Crystal Mountains, who had been privy to all information, both about the progress of every community on the remote continents and everything relevant from Earth and beyond. They knew the actual purpose of these isolated groups of humans and received frequent updates. Not even the Oshki observers embedded in these cultures knew the complete situation.

The Oshki, other than Mater and Pater, knew nothing of these things. They did not know their role in the plan. For them to do so would have skewed the results as much as interference on the other continents would have made the experiment useless.

Siglinde noticed Pater's stumble, and she wondered how Pater could know about old human cultures. If what he said was true, no one from Jewel had left the planet, let alone visited Earth.

How can it be so Earth like? Siglinde thought. *How can Pater know?*

They wandered into the village centre and stood beside the work pavilion. A water-well super-structure extended a metre above ground. The open village square comprised dusty sand that allowed for visible footprints.

"They can't see or hear us," Pater said and pointed to the dirt, "but we are solid objects. See, we leave tracks."

"Isn't that bad?" Siglinde asked.

As if to confirm it, a child approached and stared at the strange markings on the ground. The visitors wore shoes with heels, while the villagers had moccasins. Pater could have masked their footprints, but the curiosity of youth had removed that option.

As the child knelt to examine their trail, a roar and a loud squeal came from beyond the far end to the plaza. It distracted the child, and before anyone could move, a great wild boar charged around the corner and into the open space. The villagers scattered, except for the prone little boy, who froze in indecision. Shouts from an unseen, pursuing hunting party grew louder behind the charging pig.

The boy still knelt directly in the path of the charging beast.

"Sammi," a woman cried from the pavilion and ran towards the lad. The boar had the advantage of speed and closed the gap fast." Sammi..." the woman wailed in despair. The visitors stood near the boy. Siglinde leapt forward, and as the boar neared, she lifted the youngster. Spittle sprayed from the beast's roaring mouth. The distance evaporated. Its wild eyes scared her, but the animal shared her fright. A mob of male hunters charged into sight. They brandished stout spears, but pursued well behind the terrified beast. Siglinde turned to flee, but the beast's snout threatened and she felt its breath.

Siglinde and the boy shot a meter into the air and the animal flew past beneath. As the frightened pair hovered, another youngster, almost a man, rushed from behind. He grasped a long stout spear with an ugly sharp point. As Siglinde and her precious burden flew high, the lad planted the blunt end of the spear firmly into the dirt, braced it with his foot and aimed the point at the boar's chest as it ran at full speed into the danger; the point sank deep and the beast's momentum lifted it from the ground. The rod bent and snapped above the boy's hand as the lad fell sideways to safety while the animal's momentum took it and the lethal blade in a gentle arc to fall beyond in its death throes. It thrashed about on its back with horrible squeals and the broken spear gyrated above the body. Blood gushed from its ruptured chest as life flowed away.

Siglinde and the boy dropped to the ground, but the villagers had seen the lad shoot up and then float to earth as if by magic, or as they later decided, the blessing of the spirit. The women charged to the frightened boy as, invisible to the mob, the three visitors flew skyward and landed twenty metres away and avoided a collision with the charging women.

"I had to do it," Ted looked at Pater. "Siglinde and the boy..."

"I know," Pater said, "but now the villagers wonder. I had to move us away, or they would have run into us and felt our bodies. They have already noticed our tracks. Their finding us would not fit the plan."

"What plan?" Ted and Siglinde asked together.

The excitement gradually gave way to preparations for the community meal. The hunters had gutted and dressed the wild boar and it awaited its turn on the spit. The fire had burned down into a bed of glowing coals. Villagers removed the roasted carcass from the fire and the women cut and distributed the meat inside the pavilion. It took four men to lift the new pig over the fire and rest the spit shaft onto its supports.

The hero with the spear found himself embraced by the returned hunters. They would celebrate his passage to adulthood and focus on the feast provided by the dead pig. Tomorrow, he would hunt with the men; tonight he would sit with the men in the feast. His rite-of-passage would not be for some time, but that would be a formality for the youngster. Today, he had become a man, a blooded hunter and his blood-spattered tunic testified to his bravery.

Throughout the afternoon, villagers paused and stared at the spot where the boy should have died. His levitation had been a miracle, and the boy assumed mystic importance for the residents. They sat him in the shade by his mother, and other children sought to sit near him at every opportunity. This disrupted chores and adults scolded these others for neglecting their part in preparing the meal. The afternoon had turned into a celebration of the boy's salvation and the bounty of the pig.

On the dusty square, everyone approached the spot, but hesitated a meter away from where the boy's footprints and those strange others with deep, squared heel-prints mocked from the dust. The marks displayed a mystery, and the villagers' intelligence and curiosity demanded explanations. Since there was no evidence, they decided they had seen a divine intervention by an invisible spirit and the strange markings were a message from the spirits. That idea required little detail, but satisfied. The stories told of this day would embellish the event and the explanation, so the village would venerate the boy as a link to the spirit world. From that afternoon, sprigs of fresh-picked flowers adorned the spot and soon a shrine would appear.

The saved boy would pass into adult a few years after his saviour, but he would forever be in the older boy's debt. Fear and victory had forged a lifelong bond, a significant thing in the tribe. The indelible connection between the spirit boy and the hunter child would mark their passage through life as bondsmen.

As the villagers shared their feast and discussion of the miracle, Siglinde felt hunger. Ted and Pater did not seem so starved, but she had eaten little all day. Adrenaline and water had sufficed, but now, with the joyous feast before her, Siglinde's stomach demanded. It had been a busy day, and she longed for a place to rest.

Pater noticed.

"Come with me," he said.

Pater led them away from the village to a secluded spot. Siglinde found a soft bed of moss beneath a large tree and drifted into semi-consciousness. They waited.

"Brother," the words preceded an elder who bore a large clay pot of stew. Pater embraced the other. They appeared of similar age, and their copper faces matched. The visitor looked the same as any of the villagers.

"Brother," Pater said, "here are our visitors, Ted of Species 2 and Siglinde, human pure variant."

The visitor hugged Siglinde and touched hands with Ted. He was the Oshki observer in this community, but in all ways he lived as a member of the tribe. The Oshki would never return to the Oshki community, but he would live his days here, with his bride and family. He felt no disconnection from the Oshki or loneliness. He had his life here, as satisfying as any he could have lived in his parent community. No one became an observer without knowing it was a commitment to a life. Artificial observations could have been done, but including real people to do it gained much deeper insight. Pater and Mater needed that connection and the observer's mind always linked to theirs.

The man extracted wooden bowls and spoons from a satchel, and Siglinde devoured the concoction of meat, vegetables, and gravy. Rough, unleavened bread came from the same pouch. This home-grown fare rivalled the best that they found on the Oshki continent. It reminded Siglinde of Earth, her mother's kitchen and her homesickness.

"You can't beat home cooking," Siglinde said.

Pater felt her longing.

"My dear," he said, "you must be patient. You will return, but not right away. Events on Earth must progress first. Earth must be ready for you and the gift of knowledge you will bear."

Pater refilled his bowl and smiled.

"You speak English," Siglinde said to the stranger. "What is your name?"

"I speak many languages, and please call me Eldon. In the village, I am the patriarch and called 'the old one', Eldon, for short."

Eldon laughed at his play on the English words.

He seems to be the Pater of the village. Siglinde thought.

"In the village, I am revered for my poetry," Eldon said.

"They respect you for more than verse," Pater added.

"You know each other," Ted said. "Is the village aware of the Oshki?"

"Eldon is Oshki, while the others are not." Pater said. "Only he knows of us. There are others spread among the tribes, and with the farming community you met."

"So, Eldon, you control the tribe as Oshki." Siglinde said and anger flashed from her eyes. She did not appreciate what she thought to be an unethical domination.

Pater and Eldon's laughter did not soothe Siglinde.

"We don't control," the men said as one.

"We simply observe." Pater said. "The village here, as with everywhere you go, including among the Oshki, is free and develops in their efforts. There is no guidance within the plan. We simply watch."

Pater had gilded the truth. They all did more than watch, but they carefully avoided any interference that would skew developments. Occasionally, they inserted a suggestion or idea to stimulate, that was partly the need for Eldon's verses, but they would not guide. All the tribes and agricultural village on this continent had the same interaction. Only on the third continent they had no embedded observers. It would be too dangerous. That culture had to play out in its unaltered way with remote observation. It would help to understand Earth's European cultures and development from a few centuries before. As ghastly as the situation was in those third continent communities, interference could not happen. The lid had to remain on the petri dish.

"The boy you rescued will have great power because of your miracle," Eldon said. "I will mentor him in the old ways so that he will lead in the right direction. Power without empathy can lead to disaster. His saviour will become a powerful hunter and leader. That could threaten the stability of the community, but the tribe has traditions to deal with self-important individuals. I will guide him to ease any conflict."

"I will answer all questions about our people," Eldon said."

Siglinde noted the inclusive "our" and looked more closely at Eldon.

"Your people," Siglinde asked.

Pater and Eldon exchanged glances.

Is it time, Eldon's thought came to Pater.

It must be so, Pater thought in return. *A star-ship of Species 2 approaches with a human and a hybrid. Ted and Siglinde and the one called Liz are intelligent and suspicious. It is time we allowed them to understand.*

"Siglinde, Ted," Pater began. "Finish eating and we will talk of Jewel, of the grand enterprise of Jewel and the hope of the plan."

Chapter 14

Flotsam

"The first time ever I saw your face."
-Evan MacColl

The black woman, knelt over another, copper hued beauty. Liz had opened Anya's shirt and leaned towards the prone woman. Her overlapped hands formed a compression between the victim's breasts, and she pushed down hard, released, pushed, released and all the while singing the words to a dance tune that had survived the decades:

"And we're stayin' alive, stayin' alive Ah, ha, ha, ha, stayin' alive, stayin' alive Ah, ha, ha, ha, stayin' alive..."

Liz had swayed to the song many times on Earth. They had taught it in Emergency First Aid to time CPR chest compressions. She could never have imagined that the song might one day pace her desperate efforts to help save the life of someone she loved.

...push, release, push, release, stayin' alive, stayin' alive, push...release...push...release...stayin' alive...

"Don't die on me, love, don't die." Liz cried.

Liz stopped and pinched Anya's nostrils and covered the woman's mouth with her own. She puffed air into Anya's lungs. Her chest rose, good sign, and again.

Liz did not know how long she repeated her efforts. Her crying heart said forever, but it took five horrific minutes.

Anya awoke and felt Liz' mouth on hers. Liz' finger and thumb pinched Anya's nose. Anya felt a burst of warm air into her mouth and lungs. Liz' mouth disappeared.

"Wake up, damn you," Liz's voice broke and tears washed her cheeks and dripped to Anya's face. "Don't die on me, love."

Anya twisted sideways and coughed out a trickle of water.

Liz shouted in joy.

"Easy, girl, you scared me."

Anya struggled to sit. Liz eased her down onto her back and rolled her gently onto her left side.

"Rest a bit, baby, just rest."

Liz cradled Anya's head and gently drew strands of wet hair through her fingers. Tears dripped onto Anya's cheek. Liz's hair looked no better, as if they had survived a shipwreck. In fact, they had endured the stormy wreck of their outrigger and washed ashore on the beach at the base of the Crystal

Mountains. Anya breathed rapidly, but gradually eased into a regular cadence.

"Where the hell did that storm come from?" Liz asked. "I thought you powerful people controlled things on Jewel."

Anya sat and frowned. She had never been to this island, but the crystals arching high above the trees told all. Perhaps the killing water was normal for this place.

"Jewel controls, not the Oshki," Anya said. "I have never seen a severe storm, let alone whatever hit us. It seemed the sea tried to kill us. It happened so fast I could not intervene to keep us safe. Fear and surprise stole my ability."

Anya stared at Liz, and the human floated slightly above the sand before gently settling again. She yelped in surprise.

"Sorry, love, but I had to make sure I could still do that. If I had had a warning, none of this would have happened, not that I didn't like your kiss."

"It's called the kiss of life." Liz said.

"I could get used to it. It could be a kiss for a lifetime."

Both women blushed, but skin colour hid the signals. Anya had never flirted with a human, and Liz had never flirted with anyone as mysterious as Anya.

"This is a kiss for a lifetime," Liz leaned forward and softly touched her lips to Anya's lips.

"A lifetime," Anya said and returned the soft touch. "Promise...?"

"Lovers may die, but love never does." Liz said.

The pair embraced and cried. The mixture of the recent fearful confrontation with death, and a newly admitted love, astounded both women. They held each other for some time, but soon the heat of Sigma D shimmering on the beach and the discomfort of wet clothes forced them apart. They stood. Liz looked deeply into Anya's eyes, as if it were the first time she had seen her face. Her feelings overwhelmed.

"Please tell me you didn't manipulate my feelings," Liz said.

"Never," Anya said, "I promised I would never, oh my, oh...never."

Too long we have tarried
Oh, do let us get married
But what shall we do for a ring?

They kissed gently. Their happiness at finding each other's love distracted, but then Anya said.

"We have something more important to do at the moment."

"More important," Liz asked. "I think I just lived the most important few minutes of my life."

"For me too," Anya said.

The women lingered in silence until urgency brought Anya back to the task.

"There is another face you will see today. Let's go."

Anya turned towards the trees and the Crystal Mountains beyond and towards the one who they must meet. Anya had not been aware of what the Crystal Mountains really meant until just now, when Mater had touched her mind with the knowledge.

On the edge of the wood

Down the beach, in other trees, Mater stood and smiled. She had known Anya's heart ever since Liz had arrived and Liz's heart had betrayed her on that first day. Mater did not feel guilt at having hurried the inevitable. The soft blue sea had almost resisted Mater's intervention as it violated the benign essence of Jewel. Anya had never been in danger of dying, but neither she nor the human woman would discover Mater's match making. The impish hybrid RoH would have accused Mater of being a drama queen.

Just as they hoped for Siglinde, Mater saw Liz, with her love of Anya, as an instrument to bond star travellers and humanity, just as they knew the one Liz would now meet bonded Species 1 and Species 2 in accidental conspiracy. The thousand-year game of the Miigis had reached its unexpected finale. It was necessary before RoH could write the next chapter.

Time grew short. News from Earth said that both the human project and the galactic effort had progressed. Visitors would arrive soon, the first real human refugees. While the plan did not really require it, Mater knew that having Liz Siglinde understand the galactic reality would help to lead humans into the stars. She had an optimistic view that humans would choose correctly defeating the dismal odds that Ted and Species 2 had calculated. Species 2 did not understand the power they had unleashed in creating Ellie, and that power, the wonderful blend of human empathy and alien calculation, would be the key. In the same way,

Mater and Species 1, the Miigis had not appreciated the reality of RoH.
    Liz was about to learn part of the truth.

Chapter 15

The hills are alive...

*They dined on mince
And slices of quince
  - The Owl and the Pussycat*

Liz found the walking too easy when they emerged from the narrow band of forest between the beach and the first jagged cliffs. She decided that someone had created the path from the beach. As the sound of surf faded, they reached precisely cut stone steps and climbed between unbroken crystal walls that soared towards the sky.

Although from a distance they had looked like slivers, massive crystals enclosed them in a shimmering world. The cliffs soared skyward and disappeared into the blue. The light from Sigma D danced off and through the crystalline prism of the peaks, and the dynamic kaleidoscope mesmerized. On Earth, Liz had seen similar but less impressive displays from laser light shows. She focused on her feet to avoid total disorientation.

Anya also seemed in thrall, but she led the way without difficulty. She walked with purpose and felt a compulsion, as if the rock forced her. The passage offered no choice.

The women shared one common issue. Neither understood the significance of the Crystal Mountains. If anything, Anya's surprise would exceed that of Liz. Pater and Mater had said little about the mountains, and the Oshki only saw them as beautiful objects that shimmered on a blue horizon. The Oshki often wondered about the mysterious place in a world with no other mystery. To the Oshki, the mysterious universe occupied their thoughts, and the pleasures of existing on Jewel gave enough with little thought of the crystals on the horizon.

The women followed the narrow gap between smooth crystal walls, and the unblemished crystals created an open feeling even though only a meter separated the walls. Angular, crystal facets made it impossible to see far ahead or behind as they formed a sinuous path. The surfaces reflected their images as if a fine mirror, and then as suddenly appeared to absorb all light.

Liz repeated her hardness test with the diamond ring. Her efforts left no mark, but the crystal responded by tracing her efforts in colourful lines like an elaborate Earthly touch screen. It astounded Liz when the markings changed to a strange script. Steve Jorgensen on Earth would have instantly recognized Species 2 glyphs. They would have translated as "Welcome Liz", but she had no training to understand. That knowledge lay ahead.

Anya pressed on, and time seemed to have no importance. The walk had been long enough that their clothes dried. A quiet, harmonic hum increased as they moved ahead. The musical tones surrounded them, as if the crystals sang. Liz touched a wall and felt a slight vibration. The Crystal Mountains resonated on a complex tonal scale in a beat and melody that expressed celebration and soothing.

"That music is a chart-topper," Liz exclaimed.

Anya frowned at the unfamiliar reference to modern human music culture.

"The crystals resonating in the wind," Anya said, but then frowned. Somehow, the Oshki woman knew it was not the wind. Anya took two more steps and stopped, cocked her head and Liz thought her love listened for...something, not the music. One more step and Anya collapsed. Her tears and sobbing echoed from the narrow passage.

"I can't hear," she sobbed.

"Hear what?" Liz asked, and she knelt to comfort Anya.

"I can't hear them. I can't hear my Oshki anymore, only the music."

Her sobbing grew to drown out the crystal's resonance. "I am cut off from my friends."

"Oh, please, what can I do?" Liz cried. "What could you hear before?"

Anya's sobs subsided as her mind struggled to understand.

"For all my life...all my life," Anya said. Her voice shook, and the words struggled. "I have always...we have always been able to hear each other's minds whenever we wanted. We, the Oshki, were one and of one mind. I am alone."

Her sobs threatened to return, and Anya paused for a moment.

"I could hear their thoughts on the beach, but as we came into the crystals, their minds disappeared. We disconnected. For an Oshki, it's like I am suddenly blind."

Liz hugged tightly as trembles and tears threatened her love.

"I feel so alone," Anya said. She leaned against a crystal wall and slumped to the ground. Liz had not seen a despondent Oshki since her arrival. The sobbing Anya broke her heart, and she felt more alarm than she had on the beach when she feared someone she loved would die. Somehow, the soul of Anya's existence had shattered.

"Shhh, love, I'm here." Liz dropped to her knees and took Anya in her arms. She kissed the top of Anya's head. "I am here."

Anya turned and looked into Liz' eyes. In an instant, she calmed.

"Is this what humans must do? Can do?" Anya asked. "You feel togetherness like this."

"This is the best way." Liz kissed Anya's forehead. "We always feel those we love in our hearts and remember them and keep them close in our minds. We must fill in the gaps when we next meet. You, Oshki, never had those gaps, the absences."

"No,"

"You are feeling your humanity, Anya, your connection to us Earthlings."

"Oh, I do," Anya exclaimed. "I do."

A sudden revelation hit the Oshki woman.

"I am human," she said.

"Of course you are," Liz kissed again, "of course you are. You feel the depth of bonding, joy in the other and love."

A sudden resonance of the crystals washed the women. Back in her hut on the mainland, Mater smiled. The plan unfolded.

They had chosen Anya as the first of the Oshki to progress. Her role had not yet clarified, but RoH would determine that. In the short term, Anya and Liz had much to learn.

> *And hand in hand*
> *On the edge of the sand*
> *They danced by the light of...*

The crystals shimmered wildly, far exceeding their earlier glow. Internal light joined the brilliance of Sigma D and the combination cascaded in showers all along the path. The sparkling cliffs seemed to dance in celebration.

Of what, Liz wondered.

"Oh" Anya exclaimed.

"What," Liz asked.

"I hear a voice in my head, someone, alone, ahead."

"Who?"

"I don't know," Anya said.

They hurried forward. Waves of crystal brilliance drew them along the way. The women felt urgency and a closeness for the goal. Anya and Liz burst from the trail into a huge open area. Liz experienced the dissonance that she felt once when emerging from a dense jungle into a cleared village in Papua. The space was enormous and dislocating after the confinement of the cliffs. She saw no village, but a short distance away, a lone figure rested on a bench made of pure quartz. The other difference from Liz' jungle village was that the figure was not human. The being had a grey-blue skin that shimmered slightly in the crystal light. He looked like Ted, the actual alien Ted, a Species 2 alien. Liz had no other alien species to compare.

Anya stopped abruptly, and Liz crashed into her. Only Anya's ability kept them from falling.

"That wasn't a dignified way to meet a stranger," Liz said.

"Greetings," the alien said in perfect English. "I hope this means I can go home."

The alien glanced at the sky. Liz felt alien eyes could not convey emotion like humans could, but the lingering gaze made her wonder. She felt their longing.

What, Liz thought, startled by the clarity of the sensation. *I felt his loneliness. What is going on in my head?*

"Who are you?" Anya asked. She knew the entity was of Species 2, but she had never met them. Its biologic gender was male.

"Ted, is that you?" Liz asked. She trembled, still from the clarity of her brief connection to the alien mind.

Siglinde told me of her conversation with RoH in Charlie Keys' kitchen. Liz remembered. *She said RoH entered her mind and made her see and believe things, but Siglinde said she was not consciously aware of RoH's presence. I felt his mind, his thoughts. That's different from Siglinde's experience.*

Despite her time on the ship and skill in anthropology, Liz found it difficult to differentiate individuals of Species 2. She had learned to recognize Ted in his alien form and this entity resembled her friends on the ship, but she realized this individual was not quite Ted. One had to recognize the subtle differences as biologists learned the notches in a whale's tail.

"Oh, not Ted, but who are you?" Liz asked.

The catastrophic sound of his alien name did not shatter the Crystal Mountains, but echoed through the many valleys between the peaks. Liz trembled. Anya remained calm and returned his comment in a guttural explosion of Species 2 speech.

"Where's Steve Jorgensen when I need him?" Liz joked. She had only seen Steve in video as Ellie Keys', the alien hybrid's lover and designated Species 2 translator to English.

"You don't need him," the alien said. "As you see, I speak English."

"Thank you," Liz said. "I doubt I would last long listening to your language."

We do not need to be verbal. The alien's thoughts entered Liz's head. The alien made a face that Liz took as a smile. Her second helping of the clarity of his thoughts startled Liz.

"I would prefer sound," Liz said. "I'm used to it, and I cannot return the favour, but how did you know about Jorgensen?"

"You may soon talk in thought. This is a mysterious place," the alien said, "but the mystery will soon be clear. Your brain is already different. I have been here for twelve of your Earth years, but I hope my isolation has served its purpose and will soon end. In my time here, I have known everything, but until now, could tell no one. Thank you for freeing me. It has been restful and allowed me to think, but I would like to be involved again."

"Here, alone...?" Liz asked. "How did you not go mad?"

The alien glanced at the crystal cliffs that seemed to wall him off from the stars.

"I have never been isolated from the galaxy, but I have not been part of my species' efforts nor of my human relations' lives for that time. All the information came to me, but I could never reply."

"Human relations...?" Liz asked.

"My daughter, you know her as RoH. I never knew her, so don't miss her as you humans miss a relative. I am not human, as you see, but I wish to know her and learn. She is..." he seemed to be lost for words, "well, she is."

Special, Liz heard Anya's thought.

Liz stood in stunned silence. She had believed that RoH and Ellie had been in frequent exchanges with RoH's father, who lived on a star-ship near Earth. This one claimed to be the father. Who had that role on a ship? It seemed strange, and Liz wondered if Ellie and RoH knew.

What the hell is going on? Liz asked herself.

"RoH's father is on a ship at Earth." Liz said.

"Yes, and no," the alien said. "Both are correct, and you will know soon. You will learn the answer." He said. "My life here has been comfortable, and I know of all that is in our collective, all events, but I am only a listener. I have no way of communicating back to them all."

"Like someone back home yelling at the television," Liz said. "No one can hear you. It would drive me crazy."

In a clear vision, Liz saw an alien body floating in a viscous bath inside a large transparent tank. It floated gently, and its eyes suddenly opened. This time Liz knew the eyes conveyed frustration, loneliness and terror.

"My experience isn't like that," the alien said. "That was on Earth and reflects the cruelty of humans. RoH sent that image some time ago. It is what she saw. I know why I am here. Why both humans and the Oshki are here," he nodded at Anya, "and you are about to find out. It is the plan, and I have always known the plan, at least since they brought me here."

The alien looked beyond Anya and Liz to another figure and gave an alien version of a smile.

"What's the plan," Liz asked, "and who are they?"

"Come with me, back to the Oshki, to hear all." Mater's voice startled from behind the women, and she strode into the space. "Come to meet the Miigis."

Chapter 16

All hail the king...

It is said that if you want to make God laugh, tell Him your plans.–**Anonymous**

With their meal done, Ted, Siglinde and Pater stood with Eldon in the clearing near Eldon's village.

"Before we talk of the plan," Eldon said, "let me tell you what my people here believe of our origins."

Siglinde perked up. Since her spoon experiment and gravity measurements, she had growing suspicions about Jewel. She had conducted her gravity check several times and had never found a deviation, even on the other continents. Jewel had a uniformity that perplexed. No natural body ever had unvarying gravity. The rational explanation, that intelligence had created an artificial moon, seemed to be more irrational than the more likely natural origin, but it remained her favourite hypothesis. The probable did not eliminate the impossible. She had, after all, watched a 200-kilometre diameter comet guided by Species 2 make a precise impact on Mars. Perhaps the village's beliefs would touch on that.

"There are several villages such as mine," Eldon said. "They share common myths and stories. One such story is the origin of the world, and they use a word for it similar to your name on Earth."

"Unlike the Oshki, who name this world, Jewel." Siglinde said.

"You might guess the ironic symmetry between the words Jewel and Earth," Pater said.

Siglinde stared at Pater. He had strengthened her thought about the origin of Jewel. The impossible threatened to escape into reality.

"The lore," Eldon continued, "says that an animal, what we call the kima, gathered falling stars and built its home. In its generosity, it allows the people to live here after rescuing our ancestors from such a shooting star about a thousand years ago. Each village has slight embellishments and differences, but it is all the same story."

"There is a psychological theory on Earth that these myths are really archetypal memories and reflect actual events," Siglinde said.

"They celebrate the creation date," Eldon said, "each year on the darkest night when Jewel is on the far side of the mother planet, away from the sun, what you call Sigma Draconis, and the high point of the ceremony is when a certain bright star is at zenith. The creator is supposed to live in that star. It is a time of feast and celebration. Villagers light a bright bonfire that night. The story claims it is then, on one of these anniversaries, that a brilliant star will descend, guided by the huge fire, and sent by our sky ancestors to take us home."

"Wow," Siglinde said, "this matches many Earth creation stories and the hope for ultimate salvation. Your people, like humans, are intelligent, curious and creative. They need to explain things, and when they don't have real understanding, they create stories as a satisfying explanation. As a scientist, I might scoff, but as a human, I find it beautiful and exciting."

"Unfortunately, that night is almost half a year away. You would love the celebration and," Eldon laughed, "the food is superb."

"We came upon a feast day for the village," Pater said. "There is not usually so much activity in the community kitchen. They believe that a great spirit guides them and that the spirit owns all, including them. It protects and teaches them, and its spirit lives in everything, living or not."

"The incident with the wild pig and the boy being rescued by invisible hands reinforced that." Eldon added. "They revere pigs and thank them for their sacrifice in sustaining the tribe. You saw their ceremony over the hog's body. The animal being involved in the miracle adds depth to the sanctity of the child's survival. Tomorrow, they will eat that pig with ceremony and reverence. This day will become a fixed feast day for the village."

"But we know it was us, not the spirit that saved the boy," Siglinde said. "Would you have intervened if I had not been there? Don't you control these people?"

Siglinde looked at Pater.

"Never," Pater said. "We only observe; we don't control events. That would ruin the experiment. We watch daily activities here, but get frequent reports. We are more interested in the historic sweep of these people's existence than the day-to-day details."

"I make those reports," Eldon said. "I am here as part of the community, but only to watch. If you had not been here, the boy would likely have died."

"That's cruel," Siglinde said. "You have the power to prevent his death. Why would you not use the power?"

Eldon sighed. Siglinde could not know that he felt sadness at every tragedy. Even as a powerful being, he could not influence outcomes. While the experiment profoundly affected the observer, he could not let the observer affect the process. He had become part of the process and that forbid him from ever using any Oshki power.

"In the experiment, sometimes the cat must die." Eldon said.

Siglinde frowned, both at the callous disregard for life and that Eldon seemed to know that quantum exploration was her scientific specialty. He even understood the famous, and often butchered metaphoric thought experiments of the 20th centry.

Unlike Species 2, Eldon and Pater's reality already possessed empathy. Eldon frequently visited the nearest Crystal Mountains to seek strength and healing. If Siglinde could peer into his heart, if she had the quantum mental abilities to read his thoughts, she would know that Eldon suffered at every tragedy. Pater and Mater were no different.

"As you saw," Eldon said, "the villagers have many human characteristics. Humans share some basic features with all sentient species in the galaxy."

"In the explored part of the galaxy, at least," Ted said.

"The entire galaxy," Pater said. His certainty shook both Ted and Siglinde.

"As you said, these intellectual characteristics include intelligence, curiosity and creativity," Eldon said. "We," Eldon swept a glance over the little group, "understand the reality of what happened in the square with the boy, and the danger. The villagers saw a magical event. Having the characteristics I mentioned, they wanted to understand and explain the incident, so without knowing the truth, they have already created a myth about it, a myth that involves the Great Spirit and reinforces that belief. It fulfills their need to explain. I'm not sure what would have happened if you had revealed yourselves, but in the end, they would have created a myth to explain it rather than accepting the facts. Only repeated contact would destroy the beliefs and lead to growth."

"We are curious about that," Pater said. "We see it on Earth with some humans. Even with the undisputable presence of Species 2 on Earth, many humans refuse to stray from myth and belief and accept reality. It would be nice to understand how that develops, and this village is part of that learning. We would rather see them develop some sort of scientific method and understanding, but that is as yet not evident."

"On Earth, the different beliefs fight each other and that leads to horrible suffering." Siglinde said. "It took thousands of years before science developed rational explanations of many things. Even now, huge numbers of humans deny reality and prefer the myths. I found it frustrating, and now with aliens on the planet, it's embarrassing us in the galaxy."

"Humans don't embarrass me," Ted hugged Siglinde.

"That is why it is important to understand that in humans. It might allow us to help." Pater said.

"We left Ellie and RoH to sort out that mess," Siglinde said. "Many of the myth believers like those who follow witchcraft, magic and astrology are harmless, even entertaining, but others are evil and capable of murder in the service to their gods."

"In our species," Ted said, "we don't consider our old mythical origin stories. They remain deep in history data banks, but the many myths and stories of Earth, and the rich culture that grew out of those ignorant fables, attracted us many years ago. All of us who worked on Earth had to review all of our old myths, along with all we knew of Earth. It gave us understanding and reduced any judgment of a primitive world that we might bring to our fieldwork. Our species overcame the danger and reached the stars. On Earth, those old myths still have many believers and much power. It is one obstacle to Ellie's work of leading humans to the stars."

"Objectivity is the same with us, and here on Jewel, but science is not all," Pater said, as if he tapped ancient wisdom far beyond that of species 2.

"Ellie must find the key to unifying belief and reason on Earth if human progress is to be saved and extended and we depend upon RoH. We have no other active species as advanced as humans to observe. Earth is the only known planet in the galaxy that is currently on the cusp of success or disaster."

"Pater is correct," Eldon said. "There is a mystery to the universe beyond the observable. This demands a flexible attitude; perhaps we could say a spiritual approach to reality. This village is part of that search for us."

"This sounds like an unethical experiment," Siglinde said. She could barely contain anger.

"Is it unethical?" Pater asked.

"We don't experiment on humans," Siglinde said.

Ted remained quiet. If Species 2 could show embarrassment, he would have blushed. The breeding line that led to Ellie and RoH qualified for Siglinde's condemnation. He wondered if she understood that. Was the unqualified success of having Ellie, and now RoH, enough to justify it all?

Ted did not know that they all, human and Species 2, were experimental subjects on Jewel.

Simplistic answers had never been satisfactory to Ted. The universe was too complex for glibness. The collective struggled with this Earth-based question, even to the limits of the furthest star system they inhabited.

"No unnatural events occur here and we do nothing magical to affect the lives of this village,"

Pater said. "On earth, unethical experiments put human subjects in danger. The same applies to all species there, but human exceptionalism ignores that lapse of morality. Your abuse of Earth's natural systems is an unethical experiment.

These people experience nothing that a similar village would not see on Earth. As a matter of fact, the environment surrounding this village and life here is much more bountiful and benign than on Earth. We want to see what humans do without scarcity and without high-level technology. We have noted they invent mystical explanations for questions that their lack of knowledge cannot answer."

"Some time ago, RoH told me that there were questions that Species 2," Siglinde hugged Ted, "cannot answer, at least not yet. RoH held hope that answers might come, but she alluded to mystical explanations that could be correct but un-provable with science. I have seen no hint that Species 2 retreats to mysticism."

"It is so," Pater said. "The search for the answer involves more than Species 2. We also search; think and some even do things you humans would consider as prayer. It is certainly meditation, but it is not mystical in some religious context. Somehow, it is spiritual, but then we, like Species 2, don't understand that well. Perhaps these tribal villagers will teach us."

Siglinde eyed Pater. His use of words implied that he was not of Species 2. She had already thought that to be true.

"Pater, are you human?" Siglinde asked.

"Somewhat," Pater said. "I am Oshki."

Siglinde turned feet apart and hands on hips.

"Stop beating around the bush," she said. Siglinde's face reddened and her eyes flashed. "Jewel is a mystery, and you know the answers. You are part of the mystery. I have no right to demand, but I need to know. I think you are separate from the Oshki."

"It's her job," Ted said to calm his lover and lighten the mood. Pater smiled. Siglinde's scowl demanded an answer. He could not put it off much longer.

"Eldon, my brother," Pater said. "You must get back to the people. I will take our friends to the northern continent, where I must reveal the plan." Pater gripped Eldon's elbow. Evening fell rapidly here, and the shadows had embraced the little clearing.

Eldon frowned at the mention of the third continent.

"Soon," he said and hugged Pater.

"See you soon," Pater said towards Eldon's back as he disappeared into the gloom.

"Come, we must leave now."

A glow engulfed the three, and they rose to the sky. Siglinde watched the peaceful village disappear with its festive fires and faint human shapes around. If they noticed the alien effects on their leaving, the villagers showed no sign.

Chapter 17

Mud and blood and steel

This trip included a sleep cycle and they arrived at dawn in an unfamiliar territory. Siglinde thought they had landed in a diorama of the European middle ages. Pater chose the crudest of peasant villages because it was near the event he wanted them to see.

"There are several similar cultures on this continent. I will take you on a holographic tour of them, but they have developed in much the same way as we will see here." Pater led them, invisible to the locals, into the rude village.

Although the locals could not see them, the three could not ignore the putrid smell. Humans and domestic animals shared the crude hovels and wattle-fenced enclosures. A large common pasture supported cattle, goats and sheep. Children dressed in skirt tunics grasped stout staves and patrolled the perimeter. They could not tell if the weapons intimidated the livestock, or the youngsters had prepared to repel predators. Boys engaged in mock fights, and the swinging staves looked as if they could kill. The thrust and parry came close to injury. These were not gentrified people, but lived in a raw, vicious scramble of reality.

Small gardens and grain fields surrounded the enclosure and ran towards a dark forest. Women, simply dressed, laboured in the gardens or near the hovel entrances. The tanned and smudged faces of the humans did not match the colour of the Oshki. These appeared to be Earth Caucasian, but the browned and dirty skin, made that unsure.

"You don't get the smell in the history texts," Siglinde said. "The peasants barely get mentioned among the murderous kings."

"All part of the luxury tour," Pater said.

He smiled at his attempt at humour, but the normally cool and in control Pater felt uncharacteristic unease. This Earth woman and her Species 2 lover had more importance to the plan than Pater did, despite his superior quantum abilities, at least in the project's part that involved human evolution and potential. No individual pure human manifested that potential more than Siglinde Hilfreich did. He dreaded the next scene that he had to show them.

"Where are the men?" Ted asked.

"Let us walk to the top of that hill," Pater strode towards a long gentle slope that rose above the crude village. "We will be clear of the smell, but I'm afraid it will look much worse. We will find the men there."

Pater seemed reluctant to tackle the slope, but it was not the hard walk that hindered him. It was what lay beyond, and the glory of the wild flowers in the meadow could not offset his anxiety.

The trio climbed into the warm sunshine. As they neared the brow, they heard the screams of anguished humans and horses. On the far side of the hill, spread out below, lay a field of violent chaos. Men, dressed like the women of the village, but some with leather jerkins, struggled in mortal, hand-to-hand combat.

Disordered cavalry forces clashed on the flank. Large flags flew amongst the carnage that ebbed and flowed more vigorously between the banners, as if capturing the pennants had importance.

Young boys beat drums, their sound muffled by the chaos attempted to convey battle orders. Trumpets blared out urgent instructions. None of the fighters could react to the futile commands from officers at the rear of both forces. In the violent melee, neither foe could move except to flail at the nearest opponent. The physical dominance of one group of men over the other would determine the result, but both armies had reached exhaustion and there were no reserves beyond the brawl. It wasn't clear which side might win.

The violence disgusted Siglinde, and she wondered how a man could kill another as he looked into their eyes. Modern warfare had become impersonal, with soldiers firing robotic missiles from computer screens or pilots releasing guided bombs many kilometres from those they intended to kill. Most modern fighters on Earth did not need to be angry, drunk, or suicidal to fight. They just needed cold, disconnected indifference to the suffering of others they would never see. On this ugly, sunlit, blood-soaked meadow, men fought with anger and fear, each trying to be the last to die.

"Why are these fighting and killing while the other two places lived in harmony, even if they had a harder life?"

"Those others are peaceful," Pater said, "because they live as sharing communities and their environment provides for their needs, thanks to Jewel. They are in energy and a resource balance with their surroundings. They only take what they need and are in stability."

"Here," Pater swept his arm towards the ongoing carnage, "this society is based on inequality and private ownership, especially ownership of land by nobles. They have limited resources and can only use energy from the biosphere and a little wind and waterpower. Jewel has no fossil energy, like coal or oil, to distort development."

"Do you see the two men in fancy uniforms surrounded by others dressed well? One owns this land, including that village and many more, and the other owns an adjacent similar property. One is trying to steal the other's land by force. The other cultures on the other continent derive their benefit by sharing renewable resources and joint possession of the land. They have the same energy and resource limits, but they have adapted their lives to that."

"Here," again he swept his hand over the countryside, "a handful of people own everything, including the village we saw and its inhabitants. Unlike the renewable basis for happiness elsewhere, they derive their wealth and power from the land and land is a fixed quantity, so they fight over it. Our observations of all three cultures are most satisfactory. I said I would show you the several similar cultures on this continent, but they all have sadly developed these murderous ways."

"Feudalism," Siglinde said.

Ted hugged his lover and tried to soothe her mind.

"It's the same on earth," Ted said. "They derive their wealth from accumulated resources other than land alone, but the rich still steal from each other and employ serfs to generate wealth and fight their wars, just as here. Since we disabled their mass-killing weapons, they must fight like this once more, with their foe in sight, and they suffer no matter what side they fight for."

Ted pointed to the madness below.

The battle progressed in bloody confusion. It had degenerated into a grisly wrestling match. Armed with clubs and short swords, large men tried to batter opponents. Smaller individuals tried to duck beneath the swinging clubs and use their swords to eviscerate opponents. Bodies, some dead, some writhing in agony, littered the ground. There appeared to be no reinforcements, and the fray degenerated into exhausted horror. It seemed this society had not yet made gunpowder.

In the final act, the finely dressed men on either side mounted on magnificent horse, slightly approached each other, saluted with flashing clean swords, rode away in opposite directions as trumpets for both sides sounded retreat and left exhausted minions to recover the suffering wounded and bury the dead. The battle had yielded no victor this day.

"Pater, what the hell is going on? What is this planet about? What are you about, and why are we here?" Siglinde's eyes spit fire. "This is ugly and inhumane. I thought you galactic gurus were above this."

"Transplanted humans populate every place we visited," Ted said. "Each community, including this one, seems to have come from different eras and cultures on Earth. It's as if we are seeing a record of human history on Earth, a living museum."

Ted turned away from the battle. If he could feel disgust, he would, and he certainly felt the horror in his lover's mind. The ugly scene went against every principle and millennia of cultural refinement that Species 2 had developed. He felt cut off from his community, helpless, and he still could not penetrate Pater's thoughts. He tried to comfort Siglinde, but Ted felt the unfamiliar need to find his relief. The horror they watched insulted millennia of learning. The irony did not escape Ted that his species had shown similar, if somewhat more subdued callousness in its decades of abducting humans and experimenting on them. RoH and Ellie Keys' teaching had made that thought possible in Species 2.

"They are of Earth; at least their ancestors were, as are the Oshki." Pater said. "We will end this cultural exploration. I share your disgust. We have learned enough and the suffering will end. We will take steps. It is time for you to know the plan. Come, we must return to the Oshki."

Chapter 18

Refugees

Ted and Siglinde arrived with Pater in front of their cottage. The ride in the ship had been brief, and the meadow landing-zone of the Oshki relieved the lingering images of horror and the stench of the peasant village.

Liz, Anya and Mater approached through the trees, accompanied by an unfamiliar member of Species 2, who had finally emerged from his twelve-year exile in the Crystal Mountains.

The stranger's presence stunned Ted. He approached the alien and changed into his star-traveller form. The pair did not embrace or even shake hands. They stood quietly and engaged the other's eyes. Ted absorbed the tale of the one from the Crystal Mountains.

I did not know, Ted thought.

They gave me no choice; the other said. *They came and took me, brought me here and enclosed me in a velvet prison. I suffered no want and heard all the discussions in our collective, but I could not reply or contribute. The time I spent there is inconsequential.*

It's ironic, Ted said, *that they did to you, abducted you just like what we did to humans.*

Not quite, came the reply. *They know us completely. There was no examination or curiosity about my makeup. It was simply necessary for me to be away. As you have imitated a human, one of them has imitated me. I believe Mater and Pater are about to reveal their plan. I hope to learn my purpose, or the purpose of my absence. Our collective does not yet know.*

The pair of Species 2 beings turned to the group. Ted reverted to Ted, much to Siglinde's relief.

For the first time, Liz saw Mater and Pater in a tender embrace.

Perhaps, she thought, *they missed each other over the past few days. I thought they were in constant mental contact and just colleagues. I wonder if they really are aliens and will revert to their true form.*

The anthropologist considered the role of physical contact between beings of such mental ability. She concluded the Oshki were more complicated than a superficial observation might suggest.

Liz did not know that the hug also held sadness. Mater and Pater knew coming events would change their lives. The thousand-year arc of their life on Jewel would change. Neither Liz nor Siglinde had noticed much affection between the pair before that instant. Liz thought their usual behaviour reflected two lab partners who had worked well together, but suddenly realized that the experiment had ended. She would soon learn how close that comparison came to the truth and yet how wrong it was at the same time. She would learn that Mater and Pater were not Oshki at all.

Pater had listened to Liz's thoughts.

"We are not totally alien," he said. "In fact, we're more human, a bit like RoH without the ingredient that makes her special. Her mother, Ellie, would be a better comparison to the Oshki, who are similar, but special."

"Come with us," Pater said. "We must go to the welcome ground. We will discuss the plan shortly, but guests arrive, refugees who also must understand the plan and know their role."

The party walked through the trees to the edge of the forest where the vast meadow that had recently welcomed the Earthlings lay beyond. The sea of flowers danced in the light breeze.

Obviously, Siglinde thought, *Jewel had set this for arriving friends.*

"Anya, who's coming?" Liz asked.

Anya looked at Mater and shrugged.

"I don't know, but Mater says they are friends of RoH," Anya said. "No one here has met them."

As if scripted, a Species 2 ship dropped from the bright blue sky and hovered near the surface. The welcoming party approached through the grass and flowers.

Siglinde had never seen a ship from this perspective. The huge craft hovered silently; it showed no lights and made no sound. She noticed that the flowers and grass directly beneath the craft flattened somewhat, but she felt no heat. Siglinde remembered all the reports from Earth since 1947 that documented scorched circular spots on the ground, and some with radiation effects. She decided that Species 2 made those on purpose, either to create confusion or to leave humanity clues to the coming contact.

Yes, came Ted's thought. *But this is not our ship.*

"What, no Robbie the Robot," Siglinde teased Anya.

"I am told these are more fragile than your thick head," Ted said, and hugged Siglinde.

"In the short term," Pater said, "you humans, and you Ted, will need to comfort these. They need healing. Jewel has located an abode beside your home, Siglinde."

"Taking care of these arrivals will keep you busy while you remain on Jewel," Mater said, "until..."

Her voice trailed off as they reached the waiting craft. Several figures emerged from an opening. The first was a member of Species 2. Ted and the one from the Crystal Mountains stepped forward and touched the new member. Siglinde noted that the entity seemed to be weak and unsure. They turned to the dark gap in the hull. Two humans emerged, a man and a somewhat younger Earth woman. She smiled and stepped forward, unable to suppress her Texas exuberance.

"Hello, y'all, I'm Lila and this is Robert."

Lila took Robert's hand and drew him close. She looked at the odd array of greeters and her eyes swept the welcoming field. For some reason, this ordinary Earthling had taken to the extraction and inter-stellar flight with less stress than Robert, the alien hybrid.

"Robert, I have a feeling we aren't in Texas anymore." Lila said. Her infectious laugh raised a smile.

Siglinde and Liz had no clue about these people. The new alien mentally briefed Ted, and he passed the thoughts to Siglinde.

"I'll be damned," Siglinde said. "RoH has sent us some dandelions."

Lila and Robert looked puzzled, but Mater, Pater and Anya immediately understood.

I am Robert's father. In honour of my love, Robert's mother, now long dead, please call me Guy. The new alien's thoughts reached every mind. *We all need comfort and healing. Lila is both a patient and our doctor. RoH first discovered her need and her empathy. It will take time.*

We will give you that time. Pater's thought penetrated all. For the first time, Siglinde, Liz and Ted felt the power and clarity of Pater's mind. Ted stared at the Oshki patriarch.

You are, Ted's thought reached everyone.

Not of Species 2, Pater replied in kind. *Perhaps we are closer to Nova Species Human, but are Miigis.* Pater hugged Mater once more.

Liz observed an exchange of looks of love. She did not know that the Miigis had learned love, the lesson that Species 2 desired from humans after the thousands of years of human contact. Their greatest teachers were the tribes of forest dwellers in central North America, and their connection remained through a structure of pure crystal quartz, a jewel in the Canadian hard rock that sat in timeless existence on Manitoulin Island in Lake Huron.

"Come," Pater turned towards the forest. The alien from the Crystal Mountains remained, watching the entrance. They had been summoned.

As the rest reached the forest, a lone alien exited the ship and stood before the first. Both beings looked identical. Then, the new arrival changed, and a Species 2 and a Miigis stood together. Their embrace was mental, not physical.

Thank you for your sacrifice, the Miigis said. *We are sorry for your isolation, but it was necessary. Our daughter, the dust that spreads new life, is of both of us, and much more than we are. You will meet her soon.*

They followed the party of the Jewelians and alien humans as they disappeared into the trees.

Chapter 19

Lab notes

"To believe in the 'greater good' is to operate, necessarily, in a certain ethical suspension."
— Joan Didion

They arrived at the cottages. A new, larger bungalow had appeared next door, with several sleeping rooms, a large common room and kitchen. The new house shared the meadow that had appeared behind Siglinde's place.

Pater led them inside the new residence.

Lila gasped. The living area duplicated her old house in El Paso, including the huge couch where Sam had moved it and where she had seduced him, before he had blown up the church and levelled that house. In her caring heart, she hoped Sam had found his peace.

Lila felt a flash of regret. Sam had been both a lover, and, somehow, the son she needed to nurture. She looked at Robert, who had occupied himself watching the two Oshki and the human women. Lila still had a man who needed nurturing. Lila doubted that she had more than motherly love for either Sam or Robert. Her love, or perhaps lust for Sam, and her empathy for Robert did not reach deeper. The last person she had come close to being in love with was Ross Holbrooke in El Paso, but Lila doubted she would ever see him again.

Pater took note of Lila's longing.

Robert thought he knew the true nature of these people, but here he experienced an unfamiliar world of care and conviviality that he had never had on Earth. He felt Lila's flush of care. Since RoH and Lila had freed his mind and heart in that church office in Dallas, and on the few days of the trip from Earth, Robert had learned to relax. Here, in this strange new world, he felt contentment. His healing had begun. His alien father, still frail, touched Robert's arm. They had spent a lot of time together on the ship. Robert's hatred had diminished, mostly because he now knew the story of his father's suffering and the love of his mother. A lifetime of hatred for both proved to be a hard thing to destroy. Lila squeezed his hand.

Son, his father thoughts came to Robert, *we both must heal.*

Lila slipped her arm around Robert's waist. She felt healing. The dark hole in her heart had disappeared. But, as rich and verdant as Jewel seemed to be, as its warmth healed, Lila longed for the dusty familiarity of El Paso. She dared not hope that she would see it again.

"Please sit." Pater did not wait and claimed a comfortable chair. Lila, Robert and Guy sat on the padded couch. It startled everyone when Guy changed into a handsome middle-aged human who mimicked the long dead actor Guy Williams, the one who Robert's mother had loved. He, the Species 2 alien, loved her and her memory. He felt that this shape honoured his long dead lover. He also understood that Robert found the alien form less than endearing, and the love for his father, Guy, had to grow in Robert's heart.

"Father," Robert said. "Thank you for loving me. I hated you for so long, but I never knew. I wish Mom were here too."

"We could arrange it," Guy said, "but it would not really be her, and we must hold the memories and not a manufactured reality. She lives here."

Guy touched over his heart, and then Robert's chest.

"Ruth lives here."

"It fascinates us that Species 2 can develop emotions," Mater said. She had perched on the arm of Pater's chair. "It is something we had not planned to explore on Jewel, but now I think we must."

"What is the plan?" Siglinde asked. She had been asking since Pater had mentioned it.

Pater and Mater looked at the Miigis, who had left the ship to join the Species 2 hermit of the Crystal Mountains.

"Our colleague will explain." Pater said.

"Please call me Father," the newly arrived Miigis said. "That is what the one you know, as RoH calls me. In fact, we are Father."

He touched the Species 2 hermit of the Crystal Mountains.

"RoH carries both of our genes, and those of her mother, who, as you know, is a complex blend of human and Species 2 and RoH is also," he paused, "Miigis."

Siglinde stared. She saw the implications, and it explained why RoH seemed to be more than her mother, Ellie was. In fact, Siglinde had suspected that RoH exceeded the abilities of her lover, Ted. Until this instant, she had not known why.

The realization that RoH was a powerful blend of Species 2, Miigis and human shook her, but the memory of the love and empathy that RoH had shared with her reassured Siglinde that RoH, probably the most powerful individual in the known Galaxy was not a threat.

"Yes, RoH is that," Father Miigis said. "When species two began their genetic experiment with humans, not even we conceived that such a being could exist. The temptation for us to meddle in the Species 2 process had power, and so we have RoH. Unlike Jewel, we could not plan her."

"What is Jewel?" Siglinde asked. The question had dominated her throughout her brief stay. "I have guessed, with some evidence, that it is artificial."

Father extended his arms with elegant fingers and thumbs and grasped the space. An apparition of the present day planet, Jewel, glowed in his hands. It vanished in an instant, but then a small sphere grew in holographic clarity. Its pure crystal surface expanded, and they saw enormous ships circulating as if they were part of some three-dimensional printer making a ball. The structure swelled rapidly and developed surface imperfections of deep broad basins and raised ridges. Sharp crystalline pinnacles appeared at the locations that Ted had described. The ships filled the depressions with pure water. All the mountains of crystal became isolated as islands, and three large dry masses appeared, but they had located them far from each other in locations so that their masses balanced and prevented Jewel from wobbling on its axis. These developed brown surfaces as soil and minerals covered them, all delivered by a succession of massive spacecraft. One continent, Oshki country, had thin soil and an extensive network of caverns and tunnels beneath. In the final step so it would not interfere with construction, the Miigis added the atmosphere.

Father raised his hands and the sphere, a perfect rendering of Jewel, floated higher and quietly rotated as Jewel did.

"It took the material from the dead bodies of three star systems to do this," Father said. "Manufacturing soil took a lot of resources and we used large amounts from Earth to inoculate the micro-organisms and other creatures."

"But there seemed to be no birds or squirrels and things until we mentioned them." Siglinde said.

"Only on the Oshki land, and even there it was an oversight based on our false-assumption that they were not needed there. We placed most Earth creatures on the other continents. It wasn't quite like your myth of saving animals from a flood," Father said, "but we brought many breeding pairs of most species. When you missed creatures on Jewel, the planet made them to your images. We already had the genetic signatures of all life on earth, so enhanced technology created mature examples in only a few hours. Of course, some of what you saw, at least at first, we created in your heads and they did not yet physically exist. Creation takes time." He paused, "but not seven days."

He laughed and Siglinde snorted.

"You may notice that there is new diversity here far beyond your requests. It has pleased and excited the Oshki. The variety has given them a new perspective about Jewel and gives us the opening to explain to every Oshki the true story as you are hearing here. We will begin phase two of the intellectual experiment here. It excites us to imagine where that might lead in our understanding of the universe. The one saving thing about this experiment is that none of the population neither Oshki nor on the other continents, are those who actually came from Earth. Those original settlers are long dead of natural causes."

"I have shown you a three-dimensional engineering rendering. While it does not mimic Earth seasons, Jewel's rotation is exactly that of Earth. The diurnal cycle was important to prevent subject disorientation, at least at the beginning."

"That would explain the creation myths," Siglinde said. "The tribal kima story especially."

"Oh, can I visit there?" Liz asked.

"We will start with another place," Mater said.

"It will blow your mind," Siglinde said to Liz.

The image quietly rotated near the side of the room.

Everyone but Pater and Mater sat stunned.

"That," said Pater, "was how the planet came to be, now for the plan."

"We conceived and started Jewel and the plan long before Species 2 visited Earth," Pater said. "We had cloaked Jewel from them for almost 1000 Earth years to prevent contamination of the experiment. That changed when we saw their ad hoc breeding effort on Earth. They will confirm that their first visit to Jewel was after Earth year 1947."

All the Species 2 aliens in the room nodded.

"The breeding was accidental," Ted said. "We had not thought of it until that crash at Roswell. RoH's great grandfather barely survived and her great grandmother's love healed him."

"We saw it as an opportunity to integrate Species 2 into possible progress." Pater said. "We Miigis have observed Species 2 for some millennia, much the same as they observed Earth over the past century. When they took Ellie, we realized the next step, and we bred her with Miigis genes and extra Species 2 genes as well."

"You pleased us with the caring way you raised Ellie, RoH's mother." Mater said.

"Her grandfather led that. He taught us some empathy and love as well." Ted said.

Pater looked at the hermit and smiled.

"We are sorry you had to be isolated," Pater said to the Species 2 recluse, but we needed direct involvement. Father had to be you to keep your community ignorant, and since RoH has Miigis genes, we needed Father to be on the Species 2 ship, and not you."

"Turnabout is fair play, as humans say." Ted said.

"I must say," Father gave a Miigis version of a smile, "that I thought I would call the shots. At a young age for RoH, I discovered I would be the one learning and following. Everyone of Species 2 became almost afraid, including her great grandfather who began it all by accident. Only her mother, Ellie, felt it all. She knew her daughter exceeded her abilities, but their mutual love made it a non-issue. Mother and daughter would travel to the end of the galaxy to protect the other. That may well happen."

Father sat back and closed his eyes. The room felt a melancholy longing, a tinge of uncertainty that approached fear. Not even the Miigis knew the future.

A stranger would think this to be a strange assembly. Four humans, a human-Species 2 hybrid, an Oshki woman, three Species 2 aliens, Mater and Pater, and one Miigis sat in a suburban Earth living room that just happened to be on a moon-planet far from Earth. None of the participants thought the situation to be anything but normal. Liz would recount in her journal that one could consider this the first of what could be a galactic council meeting, although such a formal body would never materialize. None of the group had any power to make any significant decision about galactic affairs. That lay with the two interstellar species and upon whatever humans might decide about the fate of

Earth. It symbolized the new galactic condition that three species would now freely exchange information.

"Okay, but what is the plan from before all that?" Siglinde asked. She had the bone and would not let go.

Mater took up the story.

"The Miigis have visited Earth for thousands of Earth years. We first arrived as the last glaciation ended. We watched the melt water flood many human settlements and territories. The human species might have possibilities, so we watched their response.

"We think the warmer climate had something to do with it, but we observed the dispersed tribal structures, in many places, change into sedentary agricultural groupings and then gradually develop what humans call feudalism. The results of the growth of urban civilization both fascinated and saddened us. The violent horror of humans killing humans has persisted to this day.

"We visited many places, attempting contact, and that led to human myths and legends. They saw us as gods or devils because our abilities seemed like magic to humans."

Mater chuckled and looked at Siglinde. "Most humans still think quantum effects are magic, and you, Siglinde, are some magician with slights of hand.

"You will," Mater laughed louder, "soon pull some rabbits from your hat, beginning with quantum energy."

"I'm more experienced with dead cats," Siglinde said. "White rabbits would be a crazy change."

"The first phase of the experiment involved deliberately exploiting that mystical reaction." Mater said. "The results amused and sometimes frightened us. We would not interfere, but some human reactions disgusted us, especially when they fought over who had the correct story of us visitors. We stopped visiting these and hoped that would reduce disruption and violence."

"That didn't happen," Liz said.

"The nationality you call Greek," Mater continued, "was a case in point. They described us as grotesque reflections of their kings and nobility and invented terrible stories about us, and our supposed abhorrent actions. They used a priesthood to tell these tales and tried to keep actual knowledge of us from their populations. The rulers wanted to exploit us for their personal gain. That is much like nations today trying to manage the power of Species 2 for their gain. We finally abandoned them in disgust."

"I hope we don't have to do that," Ted said.

"Many tribal cultures created more kindly stories to explain us," Pater continued the tale. "We persisted with those cultures much longer. Long before the Greeks, we integrated with one tribe more deeply, and picked a group we had not yet visited. You know them on Earth as the Anishinaabe of northeastern North America."

"The ice had retreated on that continent. When the tribe migrated inland, following the retreating ice, we guided them. We were not ready to appear, so we left shells to give them a hint in the best way.

Their language calls these shells Miigis, so we thought of ourselves as such. That word sounds a bit like what we called ourselves. In the end, we adopted the native label. They have many stories describing their journey and the rise of their land. While fanciful, these stories contain the basic facts. They have maintained consistent accuracy over the millennia."

"The Miigis historic memory begins millennia before the human species evolved on earth. The similarity between our legends, before our knowledge grew and these Anishinaabe records, astounded us. Every human tribe has parallel stories. That similarity gives us hope for Earth's humans."

"We finally appeared to the Anishinaabe once they had found a safe place in the interior. They watched the ice retreat and the floods subside to reveal more land. They made delightful stories to explain it all. Then, when some settled on an island in a great inland sea, we revealed ourselves.

"The place we arrived is beautiful. It was even so back then, although the ravages of the ice had barely healed. The site had a natural quartz outcrop. The natives used it to quarry sharp point stone, but it provided us with a natural advantage. We changed some of the pure crystals to enhance our communication. When we made Jewel, we used the same type of quartz, taken from a nearby star system, and changed it. Jewel is in constant touch with the place of the Anishinaabe, and Earth as a whole. Lately it ties us into the network of Species 2 minds. The natives consider it a spiritual place and have lived there for 9000 years. We see it as a special place.

"RoH has just learned those stories and the reality of our first appearance. Our arrival startled them at first, but we soon developed a trust. What we had seen elsewhere had so disgusted us we guided them peacefully.

"Then we began our first inter-breeding," Mater said. "Much like Species 2, it began accidentally, but then we seized it as an interesting experiment. The results astounded us. We produced no Ellies, but enhanced humans, much like Ellie's mother. It was then that the grand plan that led to us making Jewel developed. We decided we wanted to see how human cultures would develop in a more controlled environment than Earth, so Jewel came to be."

"So Jewel is a vast experiment on sentient humans," Siglinde expressed anger. "That feudal horror on continent three disgusts me."

Pater looked sad. Apparently, the Miigis had emotions that Species 2 now sought.

"We have discontinued that experiment." Pater said. "It is being directed into something more like the first communities we saw. We have removed the dictatorial leaders and taken them to a new location. We will observe how those former despots will develop as a community when they have no power beyond themselves. Their former serfs will live free, and we hope to see what kind of culture and political system they create when free to do so. There is no lack of intelligence in both groups. We hope, long term they become more like Oshki as the generations pass. Jewel will become a completely unique entity in the galaxy."

"It still seems unethical to me," Siglinde said.

"I would like to observe it," Liz said.

Pater pondered the honesty and empathy of Siglinde's thoughts. He considered Liz's desire and planned.

"We believe Siglinde that these populations lived a benign life compared to any that humans have ever experienced on Earth. All they lack is the potential to develop non-renewable resources into complex, life-destroying technology. If their minds develop in the way the Oshki have, they won't need that complex technology and its effects. Once one understands the science, and can use quantum manipulation, making technology is easy and efficient. That would leave them free to travel into space if they desired. Jewel is freer than Earth has ever been. We will not be zoo keepers."

"We also want to understand these pure human cultures." Father said. "We think that events on Earth could cause a reversion to primitive societies, at least technologically, so we want to understand those cultures beforehand. We sincerely hope it isn't a reversion to that feudal horror you saw on the third continent. For our purposes, it doesn't matter if humans revert to a non-technological life on Earth, as long as you survive as a species and stop killing life on Earth. For humans, you would like to do that but remain technical. Either is touch and go. RoH hopes, so we hope. Earth could become like Jewel, with a high-level quantum culture in one place and simpler cultures in others. That is not our goal. We would prefer that humanity becomes empathetic, fair, and peaceful and spread around the planet."

"We actually fully expect that if humans survive, and that depends on the empathetic equity I described, they will quickly harness quantum processes." Pater looked at Siglinde. "The Miigis hope the future would allow you to thrive on Earth."

"How did everyone get here? How did the Oshki get here?" Ted asked.

"First you must know," Mater said, "that I am a Miigis-human hybrid. Pater is pure Miigis. We have been lovers since before the plan for Jewel began, over one thousand Earth years ago. We lived in the community of the Anishinaabe where the Miigis first appeared. I am part of Anishinaabe."

"Mater is being modest," Pater smiled. "She is a stunning development in hybrids. Most function like RoH's human-alien grandmother, but Mater developed far beyond that. She is nowhere near a RoH, she has no Species 2 genes, but beyond an Ellie."

Liz and Siglinde gasped. In their world, Ellie was un-opposable. Liz gave Anya an involuntary hug. Mater noticed, smiled, and then frowned.

"I must apologize to you both," Mater said. "I created the storm that threw you together. I knew both your hearts, and I knew each of you hesitated."

"You mean we were a couple of chicken love-struck teenagers?" Liz said. Only Siglinde laughed at the Earth references.

"Anya," Mater said, "I especially admired your discipline for honouring the privacy of Liz's mind. I know it was a hard struggle. I thought I had to create the storm to help you both find your honest feelings and bravery. Liz," Mater smiled, "your bravery, actions and the depth of your love for Anya overwhelmed me. The storm became a little more violent than I intended. I have never made a storm before, so forgive me. I would have intervened to save Anya, but I did not need to."

"So, how did humans come here?" Pater returned to the story.

"We prepared for the Oshki first and brought some of Mater and my descendants, several generations. We have been lovers for centuries, and we could not separate them from each other or us. I confess to some selfishness there. We changed their memories slightly so that they did not remember their life on Earth. They saw Jewel as their always home. Now, generations later, that is the natural state of Oshki's memory."

"How have you prevented inbreeding?" Liz asked. She had seen cultures with complex systems for genetic mixing.

"Some had human lovers who also came. We selected a few pure humans who had the potential we sought. It has a similarity to how Species 2 picked Ellie's father on Earth." Mater said. "That has provided the mix for the past thousand Earth years. All of those original pure humans lived a normal human life and died of old age. We expect that there will be more humans visiting from now on, and that will continue the process through natural love and bonding."

Mater looked at Lila and Robert.

"Hey," Lila said, "I'm too old for babies."

"Are you sure?" Mater asked.

"Are you sure?" Robert repeated.

Lila tried to combine a frown and a smile and failed at it. On Earth, with her life experience, Lila had resolved never to have children, but here on Jewel and now, with...

Robert hugged Lila. He relished the new feeling of attachment.

Pater frowned. He knew Lila's mind and heart. The time was not near, but he knew Lila would not end her days with Robert.

"More humans will come," Pater said. He sounded sure.

"I hope they aren't more refugees," Lila said.

"Yes," Pater said, "it would mean humans failed to survive. I think they will be visitors, more like Siglinde and Liz."

"What's the history of the cultures on the other two continents?" Siglinde asked.

"Siglinde," Pater said. "Those stray near to your ethical question. The base populations were all abducted, but not in the careless style of Species 2 in the last century."

Pater frowned at Ted, who stared back unapologetically. Mistakes were not an issue of blame or guilt, but simply an opportunity to learn.

"We deliberately examined every individual, non-invasively, and brought the best from tribes in Africa, Asia and Australia. You saw an African descended community. We did the same for European villagers who had learned a simple, cooperative life. Remember, these cultures existed over 1000 years ago. These are the developed outcomes of those initial populations. The results encourage us for the humans on Earth. If technology devolves, we will see much of this and they might be as peaceful and stable."

"Since we were there, Jewel has tweaked them so that their brains could develop in their quantum strength. We want to see if that happens. Our history does not clearly record the evolution of we Miigis from organisms such as pure humans to quantum beings. Humans are the only species in the galaxy currently at that stage of development. Much of this will be new to us, and we find that to be exciting."

"Is such a low tech future inevitable on Earth?" Liz asked. "Will humans destroy civilization?"

"We see that as a possibility," Ted said. "I mean the destruction; however, we see new hope. Recent events on Earth after Siglinde and I left on our honeymoon show progress on saving humans on Earth. We will see shortly. That task is in Ellie's hands. Her daughter has a different role. As I say, we feel more optimistic."

"One reason is that we see several enclaves of human culture who may reach the needed levels of empathy and sharing so that their discovering higher quantum effects will not lead to a disaster. One of these technologies is the quantum energy exploitation process. Normally, such ability in the hands of human control as it now is would quickly lead to overheating and destroying high order life on Earth. It would be too much power too soon, as humans have with the invention of nuclear weapons."

"We saw that as a reach too far, too soon and perhaps unnatural for human evolution. The exploitation of fossil energy and the wars they fought over it became a black swan situation that sabotaged human intellectual evolution. That gave us the moral justification for neutralizing those weapons on that New Year's Eve."

"Siglinde," Ted kissed her on the cheek, "your brain is advancing with Jewel's help. You won't reach my ability, but you will function at a high level. I am going to propose..."

"Finally," Liz said and giggled. Ted scowled at his friend.

"I propose," Ted said, "that we return to a place where the population has developed to what I mentioned before. Providing them with the quantum energy generator will not lead to destruction, but will allow them to influence others peacefully. RoH had one such generator left in a remote town. We monitor that to see if the human locals abuse the availability of that energy supply. If they misuse it, we will remove it, but that is a place with no alien or sophisticated human leadership. We wait and hope, so far so good, they are basically good people, but it is an experiment."

"We are once more intervening in human development. This should not happen for another century under normal circumstance, but we think humans will be ready, at least in those places. Also, RoH loves the people she helped with that, so they get a bit more leeway."

He looked expectant.

"Okay," Siglinde said. "Wakanda, here we come, but where?"

"The farm in Goderich, we might expand to the whole town later. WE will also locate where the Ojibwe guard the crystals. There is a factory in Goderich run by friends, and we need that place to build."

"Mike Hammersmith and Charlie Keyes," Siglinde said.

"It is Ellie's home base," Ted said, "and she is the key to it all. Siglinde, you will need to be out of the way, and so will I. Our doubles are too involved in events, so we need to remain unknown.

"Oh, and another small thing," Ted seemed uncharacteristically nervous. "Will you marry me?"

"Yes," Siglinde whispered, "YES you goof. Who will conduct the ceremony?"

Ted looked skyward. "She will be here soon."

Chapter 20

Witches of the woods

We planned to spend three Earth months in our cabin in the woods. The structure would be what they called a cottage in medieval times. We travelled there via a starship short hop a few days after Lila and Robert had arrived. Pater started us on this assignment the day that we heard about the plan concerning Earth that the Miigis had created over a millennium before. Pater took us aside after that meeting with the new arrivals.

"You know you will return to Earth soon." Pater said.

I nodded my head and began to tear up. I looked at Anya, and she seemed almost as sad as I was.

"I have someone here, now," I said. Anya's hand found mine. "I'm not sure I can leave."

"You must," Pater said. "It's necessary for you, for Earth. Your presence on Earth is essential."

"Essential for whom?" I cried. "Is it for your stupid, alien manipulation? You are so arrogant. The Miigis think you are above us all."

Pater flinched at my outburst and did not smile.

"If you don't return, humans may never travel the stars." Pater said. He showed no emotion, and that made me angry.

"If the Miigis and Species 2 are examples of what's in the galaxy, why would we want to go? You both act like smart-assed second year under grads who know it all, sophomores, sophists in the best Greek way. Maybe the Greeks had it right when they made fun of the Miigis."

Again, I saw Pater flinch. He and Mater had always been so cool and mater-of-fact. Could they even understand?

"You fear losing Anya," Pater said.

It was my turn to wince. He hit me right between the eyes.

"Yes...," I had strived to be honest in my work. That confession came easily.

"Anya," Pater turned to my love, "we want you to go to Earth too."

My heart leapt in hope. Anya seemed to be stunned. Her eyes grew wide and her mouth opened. No words came. We waited.

"I have always been of Jewel. How could I be separate? I panicked when the crystals cut me off from the all, from Jewel. How..." Her words trailed off. We waited.

Pater tired of the wait.

"My sweet Anya," Pater began. I had never heard a tone of endearment from the old folks. Right in front of me, Pater morphed into a new person.

"Mater and I love you beyond words. You are our daughter, one of our first, not a favourite. We love all the children and their children, but you are special. We will miss you beyond belief, but will always be in touch. You will carry a crystal, and the Species 2 fleet still haunts the Earth system. One of our vessels will be there too. Your lover will be with you and our love as well. You will have Liz by your side, and RoH will soon deliver a needy one who Mater and I will mentor and love.

"Anya, you have been growing into this task. Your love will make it easier, and if all fails, you will return to be with us again."

"What if it succeeds?" Anya asked.

"The future will then write its story, and you will be proud and loved." Pater placed Anya's hand in mine. I felt, at that instant, that we had united as a couple as if this had been our wedding.

"Both of you take time and consider," Pater said. "I have a minor job for you both on Jewel. Liz, it is in your field of anthropology. It's actually a once in a career opportunity to observe a society that has been completely disrupted and must explore a new start. We want you to spend time with the recently freed serfs of the third continent as they explore their new situation. We are interested in how that might work. Earth is passing through the same disruption of something that had always seemed real, eternal, normal and right. Here, the feudal serfs, and humans on Earth, are exploring a new and likely *frightening future. Please observe for us. Earth needs you."*

"Dispatches from Jewel"; Field notes of Elizabeth (Liz) Davis–Davis, E., UWO Press (Public domain)

Required reading for Introduction to Alien contact 100, G. Fontaine lecturer, S. Jorgensen supervising professor.

The morning mists lingered in the trees and waited for the sun's warmth to draw them to nothingness. Bird song greeted the day while the faint buzz of bees softened through a flowered meadow. Smoke wafted from the crooked chimney of a small, rude cottage. Whitewashed wattle walls supported a thatched roof where the dew lingered to reflect rays of early sunshine and made a silver blanket as the damp evaporated. The place seemed old, but it had appeared overnight.

"Good morning, love." Liz smiled and swung a cast-iron kettle away from the hearth's heat. "Do you want some tea, Anya?"

The quaint cottage and embracing forest created a strange setting for a scientific laboratory. Although rustic in appearance, the place had some advanced features. No one could open the battered wooden chest in the corner without the right thumbprint, or with Anya's mental ability. It hid Liz' electronics for field notes. They had no need for communication devices. Mater and Pater could follow everything whenever they wished. Anya remained in constant touch. Jewel protected them in the building. The cottage could just as easily be an Oshki dwelling, but the quaint appearance created safety in the unlikely event of discovery. An invisible barrier hid the cottage from any casual observer. It copied the system that isolated the landing zone. Mater and Pater had sent Anya and Liz to observe the recently freed serfs. The Oshki were eager to hear the observations of the Earth scientist. Mater and Pater had participated in the design of the experiments on Jewel, and they might not overcome the resulting biases. The observations would take time.

"So, we have been watching for two days," Anya said. "What have we seen?"

"I noticed two things," Liz said. "The villagers spend a lot of time working; I think carrying on their normal activities of living. They tend the livestock and gardens. They also spend a lot of time talking."

"They want to understand what happened to their masters," Anya said.

"This is an interesting scenario," Liz said. "The old power structure of feudal domination has suddenly ended. Even though their world has changed, they carry on in their daily activity, living what they see as a normal life. It seems the higher power contributed nothing to their existence, and its disappearance has not had an immediate impact.

"There is a lesson here for Earth and humans. While I watch these people, I am thinking about how Species 2 has begun a similar process on Earth, but in a slow, evolving way. Taking away the military power of countries seems to be like the Miigis removing the feudal lord here. It excites me, and I hope to gather much more data. When I get back to Earth, I'll need to talk with Ellie Keys."

Anya briefly frowned. Liz had stirred her trepidation for her pending trip to the more primitive Earth and away from the all of Jewel. She looked at Liz and love brightened her mood.

"I hear it all." Anya said. "They have much grief. Several of the men died in that battle and the wounded need much care. Without nursing and doctoring, they will probably die."

"Can we help?" Liz' empathy revealed.

"Will interfering wreck the experiment?" Anya asked.

Liz rushed her reply.

"Suffering is worse than losing the data. I cannot allow that. On Earth, they would ban this kind of indifferent experiment. Of course, the scientific community would reject the whole concept of Jewel as unethical. If I'm in the field on Earth with a villager and they get hurt, I don't step back to see how the villagers will react. I damned well help and have done it before."

"Siglinde raised that earlier." Anya said. "Her concerns led to changing this culture, what we came here to see; the project that grew from that. It may help humans on Earth."

"I think the Miigis have the wrong idea about that." Liz said. "Humans are creative and both inventively destructive and constructive. What we see here may play out in some parts of a collapsing Earth, but not in others. At best, this might be a benchmark for what happens in a friendlier environment."

"Like Goderich, where Siglinde will live." Anya said.

"I have never been to the farm," Liz said. "I want us to go there first. If RoH's heart is anywhere in the galaxy, I know it is at that place."

"One thing here that differs from natural conditions on Earth," Liz said, "is that Jewel does not have resource constraints like all cultures do. Earth must achieve a balance between the demand for needs and the resources available. That basically means the energy obtainable. Population, consumption and resources must be in balance. At one time, and in many other species, resource availability drove population. Natural forces on Earth control populations with horrible methods like starvation and disease. Humans have reached a phase change in that, but now population drives resource depletion and environmental degradation. We need to find an empathetic and fair solution on Earth."

"You think we are wasting our time watching these people," Anya said.

"No, I think this is fascinating and may be useful, but I cannot tolerate allowing suffering. If these were lab rats, I would still pamper them, but these are humans. I can't stomach their suffering."

Anya paused. She contacted Pater and Mater. It was their decision, but she told them she and Liz would not stay if they could not intervene. The problem for the Miigis lay in deciding how to provide aid without distorting the natural progress in the culture's development. This minor issue on Jewel reflected the greater problem of how much intervention star travellers could do on Earth. Events, the comet Clavette hitting Mars, had driven those considerations into unplanned directions. Humans, in their mad scramble of conflict and desire, could not know that the star travelers, ones who humans thought to be so powerful and certain, had entered an unfamiliar place of uncertainty and doubt. Species 2 had never felt such confusion despite their coldly intellectual power. Just by existing, the human species had disrupted the comfortable galaxy.

The decision to help required logistic changes. Since the women would reveal themselves to the inhabitants, they must blend in. Simple dress of linin and leather would look suitably local and replace the Oshki jumpsuits. Their headgear would mimic the natives' linen, tied down bonnet.

Local children solved the problem of how to enter the village without appearing as suspicious strangers. Once the protective shield disappeared during the day, anyone could see the cottage. Like normal village life on Earth, children explored the edges of the place. That happened here, and several youngsters approached the cottage while searching for mushrooms in the transition between meadow and forest.

Liz and Anya exited the doorway, dressed in their new rustic clothes and ready to observe the village, when excited cries came from the shrubs in the boundary between the trees and the meadow. Children might have enthusiasm, but strangers were always suspicious. Superstition and stories of witches formed part of the common lore. They scuttled among the bushes, observed the two women, and tried to remain hidden. They could not know that hiding from Anya was not possible. The women stepped into the open.

"Hello," Anya said. The children did not understand her modern version of English.

"Alheil," Anya said, "we frenden."

"Frenden?" several youngsters asked.

"Frenden," Anya said.

The tantalizing nearness of strangers, of something new, affected the children. Curiosity overcame superstition, and they eased towards the cottage and the strange women. It struck Liz that the youngsters showed little fear. She remembered many African villages where laughing children had been the first to celebrate her arrival.

Perhaps the life of feudalism makes these youngsters more cautious. Liz thought.

"Alheil," Anya repeated as the space between her and the children became more intimate.

The mob of youngsters stopped a few meters away. Their smiles held, but their eyes asked questions.

The avalanche of sound from the children, questions and greetings, sounded to Liz as some form of Middle English. Anya confirmed it. Liz imagined the mob in a Shakespearian theatre pit accosting the actors on stage.

Liz found the words strangely understandable.

"Who-so you come?"

"Wher-of from?"

"Welcomen..."

"We are friends of the Fox." Anya said. "Frenden fox."

The discussion of how to reveal themselves to the village had raised a problem. They needed a way for the villagers to accept their presence without fear. The solution resulted in a compromise.

A legend that persisted among the several villages in this shire was of a benevolent outlaw nicknamed "The Fox" since he led a cunning band, never seen and opposed the now absent Lord of the land. The idea had some risk since the uneducated villagers feared The Fox despite there being no stories of his band ever hurting or stealing from the commoners. To these simple peasants, the legend was true, and the Fox roamed. Most stories told of The Fox helping villages.

The children accepted the tale, but convincing the adults would be harder. The sudden appearance of a cottage in the forest implied magic, and there were darker tales of witches in forest lairs. These strange, formerly unknown women with unfamiliar skin colour raised suspicion. The village women felt maternal distrust of anything that threatened their families. The youth and beauty of the two visitors raised more mistrust. Witches were old hags or seductive vamps who would steal their men with magic charms.

It did not help that the sudden disappearance of the noble landowner seemed supernatural, and the most popular explanation relied on magic and spirits. Two enigmatic unattached women suddenly appearing fed that account.

The children led the women into the village with shouts and smile as if they had discovered a great treasure. This was indeed a triumph for these over the other less-fortunate youngsters. In the complex world of childish prestige, this was the definitive victory of a lifetime.

The adults proved to be more cautious.

A late middle-aged woman approached with caution.

"Al-heil," she said. Unlike the children, her lips smiled, but her eyes held distrust.

"Hello," Liz said. Her experience saw the unfamiliar word as a standard greeting.

"Wher-of jou from?" The woman glanced beyond the strangers towards the forest. Her eyes filled with suspicion.

"Yes," Liz guessed at the question. "We are from the forest."

The woman frowned at the unfamiliar language.

"Wicch," she spat the word.

"No-kinnes," Anya said. Her ability allowed her to read the woman's mind. Anya would not implant a deception, but she felt the shaky ground if they could not convince this woman of their friendliness. The person had assumed the role of greeter and interrogator.

Liz realized Anya's better perception and let her lover do the talking. She guessed that if the villagers suspected the un-holy relationship between the women, things would become violent.

"Peple neigh-goinge you-self," Anya smiled.

The woman visibly softened, but her eyes still questioned. Anya knew this would be an uneasy relationship. A shout from the gathering crowd of adults released the tension.

"Isellen, welcomen with milthnes," a friendlier woman stepped forward and clasped the hands of the strangers. "Welcomen..."

"Inca..." the first woman said.

"We mean no harm," Anya said. "No inca..."

"No inca," the second woman repeated. "Infolwen..."

The woman turned and led the strangers and the mob of women and children towards a rude hut.

Liz felt sure that Anya could keep them safe. The larger plan needed the villagers to accept them and reveal what was happening. Liz would rely on Anya to pass on all the information. She recorded everything. Later, Siglinde would make sure that Steve Jorgensen, back on Earth, received the audio. Genuine spoken Middle English would be almost as exciting to the linguist as the audio discord of spoken Species 2 language.

"They are suspicious," Anya said. She did not stop the villagers who would not understand modern English from hearing. "We must not spook them."

They passed a man prone on a litter of canvas and straw. He groaned and a bloody wound seeped through a dirty linen. Anya stopped beside the suffering man.

"He must be a casualty of the last battle and has come home to die."

Her quick appraisal showed that the visible bleeding gash on one arm would eventually kill him either from blood loss or gangrene, but she found many internal injuries only hinted at by severe bruising from some blunt weapon.

Anya could have healed him quickly, but that would reinforce the suspicion that she and Liz were witches. She knelt beside the sufferer. Anya would need to apply quantum effort, but she must disguise her ability so that it would not appear as magic.

"Water, brenning water, hihful..." Anya spoke as if a command. She needed both clean water and some alcohol for disinfectant. Both appeared. She intended this to be a lesson in medical care to prevent infection. In reality, she would use her ability to cleanse the wound beyond the dilute alcohol's effect. She could fix the deeper damage without notice and leave the seeping wound, now cleansed and subtly cauterized to heal normally. The villagers would see no magic. By nightfall, Liz and Anya would have helped a dozen battle casualties and salved many minor wounds from daily work.

Their efforts earned a feast, at least the best the village could offer. One woman played a sort of harp and many sang unfamiliar songs in rough but pleasing harmony.

"This seems like rare talent in a peasant village," Liz said as she listened to the competent melody. She recognized none of the tunes.

Anya explored the musician's mind.

"She frequently worked at the manor house and the lady of the manor had befriended her and taught her to play. Apparently, the noble woman lived a boring life, only a little less subservient to her husband than his serfs. She and this woman had spent many pleasant hours together."

Liz examined the player. She seemed slightly better looking than the others, but Liz realized her more careful care of her hair and clothes had made the difference. None of those differed from the other women, but just touched with slightly more care.

"I want to ask her about that and how she feels about the disappearance of her friend," Liz said. "I'm curious how that friendship and its loss affected her."

"I have examined her mind," Anya said. "She is honest and has a gentle attitude, but she grieves at her loss. Honesty is common here, but the hostile one who met us is a little less open."

In this pleasant ideal, a small group of villagers harboured suspicions and fear. For the moment, this would not be a danger, but the visitors wished to interact for some time and observe. While the pleasant women might learn to be closer to the visitors, the longer they stayed; the suspicions and jealousy would grow among the hostiles. Many of the old fables focused on evil spirits first earning trust before a horrible betrayal of people. In the population's ignorance, such ideas could lead to dangerous action.

The daily habit of the village required bedtime at sunset. As the shadows deepened, Liz and Anya bid farewell and returned to the cottage. Their childish escort hurried home before the horrors of the goblins of darkness might snatch them. Tales of evil spirits and wood-elves had been a common parenting tool to keep children from straying and becoming lost in the forest. Unfortunately, many adults did not outgrow those fables.

Anya and Liz brewed tea and ate a delicious pastry. Cottage life held new experiences for the Oshki woman. They had no mechanical to serve them and the experience of normal Earth activities pleased her. They settled onto a comfortable couch and snuggled.

"How did you so easily understand these people?" Liz asked.

"Aside from entering minds and learning intent, this is an old version of your English language." Anya said. "Remember, the Miigis visited Earth for thousands of years and well documented the Middle English language. I checked with Pater. People removed from what you now call England populated this part of the third continent. Pater says it was the best example of that life and a sample of the worst of your classic feudal system. They have been here as long as the Oshki, but they did not grow. Now, with their society disrupted, we will observe change, for better or worse."

"That makes sense," Liz said. "If they had no outside stress or opportunity, say discovering colonies or running out of firewood, both of which happened in Earth European history, there would be little pressure to change. On Earth, horrible plagues and clear cutting led to the collapse of classic feudalism. Now that you removed the nobility, I think there will be significant change. I'm betting on it being for the better."

"Ted's group only abducted individuals for short-term examination and then returned them, most of them traumatized. It's a struggle for me not to see the Miigis as monsters. You abducted entire villages."

Liz sipped her soothing night-time tea.

"Don't see the Miigis as monsters. On Earth, they helped and observed and did not hide from humans. The ignorance and superstitions of humans provided enough cover. In addition, the plagues you mentioned killed entire villages. The ones we took just seemed like that had happened to them. They actually benefited from being saved from a horrible death."

"Species 2 had to deal with a more sophisticated and dangerous population that had fusion weapons. That required the more blatant intervention that you witnessed. The Miigis are, like all the star travellers, detached when interacting with other life, sentient or not. Humans do much worse in how you treat other life with zoos, marine-lands and circuses. Some of that life is more intelligent than humans know. Zoos and laboratories are cruel realities for them as opposed to Jewel. Every human here has a life no worse than they lived on Earth and many much better. Jewel is not a zoo.

"I admit," Anya said, "Miigis indifference allowed this feudal experiment to go longer than it should have. Field notes from Earth would have been enough. Now, though, we have created a situation never seen on Earth before. Removing the nobility here is like Species 2 disabling all high-level weapons on Earth. What we see here, post-feudalism will parallel future events on Earth. I suspect neither will be smooth and without suffering. We hope the outcome will be of significant benefit to the people, here and on Earth."

Liz remained thoughtful. The ethics of anthropology study on Earth did not allow for intervention in any community. They would think that the creation of isolated, ideal populations as abhorrent. The effort might look like Huxley's Brave New World. It actually would make results useless. Earth scientists did not have a benign place like Jewel to allow for humane and yet useful study of humanity. Although, she admitted that galactic overseers by neutralizing strategic warfare had turned the whole of Earth into a glorified and potentially beneficial rat labyrinth. Liz realized that mice and rats might think the same way about human experiments.

"I notice you refer to Miigis as if they are separate from you, Oshki." Liz said.

"They are." Anya said.

Liz noted she had raised her voice and knew Anya had an emotional depth. Her love had been slightly upset since Pater had explained the plan. Liz suspected the revelation that Pater and Mater were not actually normal parents. had assailed Anya's heart. She squeezed Anya to her and kissed her forehead.

"Yes," Anya said, "we Oshki are part Miigis, but we are also human. Like Ellie, like RoH, we are a new entity. It joins us to both species, but still makes us a new entity. I do not know what that might mean."

Children did not escort them to the village the following day. The people had gathered for a religious service. The visitors remained in the obscure back of the congregation. They saw symbols of Earthly Christianity, but they could not identify a priest. A man in crude every-day clothes stood at the front on a low platform.

Although dressed as a field worker with no hat, the leader had a colourful scarf draped around his neck and hanging down in front. He stood at a rough dais that resembled a tall, crude wooden barrel. He held an ornate, unopened book in his left hand and gestured with his right as he spoke.

"God with-al you," he chanted. The worshipers responded in kind.

The man's chants musically resonated. Responses followed in what Liz thought of as a long practiced ritual. The massed voices surprised Liz with their clarity and perfect tune. Unlike some modern church services that Liz had observed on Earth, the congregation projected enthusiasm.

At one point, the leader or priest, Liz thought he would be called a lay-leader on Earth, dramatically waved the book, but he did not consult it. He seemed to work from memory and stumbled occasionally, as if he had misquoted or remembered an omission.

"I don't think he can read." Liz whispered. Anya nodded.

After the rituals, no one left the gathering. The leader preached, and a lively discussion followed. Group members stood and talked, and then another contributed.

"What's going on?" Liz asked. The village version of English would take time to become understandable.

"They are discussing their new situation," Anya said. "The noble's disappearance confuses them. The majority attribute it to their God, or some devil."

"I don't like the looks we are receiving." Liz said. "I wish I could understand."

Instantly, Liz heard the people translated into modern English.

"How..." she asked.

"I'm sorry, my love, but I have entered your mind to feed their words translated through me. I thought it would help, but if you want, I will withdraw."

"Go ahead," Liz said. If she could not trust the woman she loved, there was no love.

Anya squeezed her hand to acknowledge that bond of hope.

"So far, those who fear us are a minority. I don't think they are a threat for now." Anya said.

A debate started, and people became loud and agitated.

Someone raised the question of how to organize until the Lord of the land returned.

"I don't think our lord will return," the musician from the night before spoke. "I returned to the manor, and all has disappeared, the house and all the people. It feels like an evil place now. We must avoid it and keep the children away."

The crowd shuddered and exploded in random expressions of wonder and fear.

"As a male," the man on the platform raised his voice to intervene, "and your worship leader, it should be me. Men have the God given right to be in charge."

The worship leader tried to seem larger on the raised platform. Liz giggled at the effort. None of the villagers stood over 180 cm, although every adult, male or female, appeared to be work-hardened. The rest of the villagers did not seem impressed.

Hiltlin, the suspicious woman who had first greeted the strangers, then spoke. Her words came as shouts.

"Thom, we respect your worship leading, but men do not have any such right. Women have the right of numbers here, and we should prevail."

"What do you mean?" Thom asked.

"Look here," Hiltlin swept her hand over the group. "We are many women and a few men. Too many have died in battle. We would value you as the oxen, and we be the plow masters."

"No, no, no..." several males protested.

"The book," Thom the waved the tome in the air, "says we have the right."

"Read it," Hiltlin demanded. She threw the ultimate humiliation at the man who, as Liz thought, could not read. He glowered and struggled to find words.

"You men are still good for bed warmth and giving us with child," a woman shouted. Laughter in alto and soprano echoed.

"So who of you would lead?" Thom asked. His embarrassment had drained his enthusiasm.

"Me,' Hiltlin rushed to the platform to stand beside Thom. While she did not exactly tower over him, she had a few centimetres of height advantage.

"I'm not sure that her being in charge will be good for our stay," Liz said. Anya squeezed her hand.

"We will be fine as long as we stick together where I can protect you. I hope that won't happen."

It startled Anya when the friendlier woman from the first day shouted that Anya, or "the consoling bede-woman" or the healing woman as she described Anya, should lead. She argued that Anya had done great work and would be neutral.

"How dare you want walkirie," shouted Hiltlin from the platform, labelling Anya a sorceress. She glared at the visitors with hatred.

Anya did not want to be their leader, but she wanted to see how the debate developed.

After a heated exchange where someone pointed out that they did not really know the strange women and Anya did not know the village, the gathering appointed the bully-woman as Wissere. Liz thought she was a tyrant and often got her way.

"This is exciting," Liz said. "I get to observe the start of a community's attempt at creating a new political organization. I must make detailed notes and keep watching and talking with people. Pater never envisioned this."

"The Oshki have no structures of governance at all," Anya said. "Even this bit is inconceivable, but they lack our communication advantage."

The resulting organization was as simple as possible, meaning they created no legal body. Wissere Hiltlin would function in the familiar way that the Lord of the land had ruled.

Liz wondered if the lack of formal rules would develop into a new feudalism or lead to eventual rebellion. The first might show some insight into what had happened on Earth 10,000 years ago when feudalism evolved, or what might have happened if tribal structure prevailed.

Liz recalled the Hebrew fable of Cain and Able, which suggested that the change from tribal herding to urban feudalism was a violent civil war. Perhaps, this time, Able would kill Cain, and in that case, she predicted that the bully, Hiltlin, and her feudalism would not live long. Liz felt guilty being the detached scientist, and despite not liking Hiltlin, she could not wish her harm.

"It isn't my field of expertise," Liz said, "but I wonder why the anarchy of tribalism evolved into ridged, top-down feudalism. From what Ellie Keys said, the aliens think humans have to reverse that."

"I must learn from you," Anya said. "I do not know about repression and the use of selfish power."

"If you come with me to Earth, you'll get a belly full of it, and believe me, it'll give you a tummy ache."

Liz laughed and left Anya with more puzzlement. She did not get the joke. Liz noticed.

"You can peek," she said.

Anya followed Liz's thoughts and laughed. Liz had to resist hugging and kissing her love. That, no doubt, would cause the villagers to riot, want to kill them and end their work here.

The gathering dispersed to daily tasks. Children went to the animals in the field, some of the young and most of the women worked the gardens and other food related work while the few men not injured in battle went into the forest to harvest firewood.

The days passed in the tranquillity of routine, and the two visitors watched. A calm stability descended on the village. They had fought the recent war in the time between planting and harvesting. The ingathering approached and the flax, wheat, oats, rye, beans and barley neared ripe. Large amounts of cabbages, onions, peas and beans had to be picked.

Pigs rutted in an enclosure that would be next year's garden.

While the village appeared quiet, Wissere Hiltlin quietly built her power beneath the calm. A small group of supporters formed around her, and even her adversary for the leadership, the preacher, joined her. Hiltlin resented Anya's popularity and decided she remained a threat. The villagers knew Hiltlin worried more about her prestige than she did about the village economy or the suffering casualties of war.

Anya continued to heal injuries. The suffering victims of the fighting seemed to make a rapid recovery. Anya paced the healing, but she lessened each man's pain while allowing their bodies to recover naturally.

Liz and Anya always stayed close together. They worked in the gardens with the villagers and listened to the conversations and gossip. That gave them a new understanding of the village, and they decided these people were ignorant, but not stupid.

Unfortunately, one of the intelligent ones was Hiltlin. Liz noticed that one woman always seemed in earshot of the strangers. She decided that Hiltlin had sent a spy. Anya tried to calm Liz' fears, but Liz could not relax. Other than spying on them, nothing happened.

Despite Hiltlin's attempts to establish a rigid hierarchy, the villagers developed an ad hoc system of operating, and the majority ignored, or at best followed, Hiltlin's desires with resentment. It did not gain their support that Hiltlin did little work, but spent her time planning more restrictive rules based on their religious beliefs and delivered each meeting day by the preacher. Most of Hiltlin's efforts seemed to be to enhance her self-importance.

The pair heard grumbling and gossip in the gardens, and when they accompanied the children in the fields and sometimes at play, they heard a more honest opinion of Hiltlin along with whispered disdain for the preacher who, after all, proclaimed himself to be the messenger of God. Liz believed the children only repeated what they heard from their parents. The popular opinion varied from disgust to hatred.

One thing that they noticed no matter where they were, the same person, a woman, always seemed to be near, pretending business, but listening. Hiltlin had developed a network. The spy could hear it all, and the innocent, trusting villagers talked freely. When the Lord of the land had control, they feared no one in their community and grumbled often against the master. They did not realize that even in the old culture, spies could be bought and some ears were dangerous. Hiltlin had been one of the lord's lackeys and understood the system.

"We should have picked our new friend, Anya. She is wise and cares for the people." Many people who disliked Hiltlin had repeated the thought.

When Hiltlin heard the reports, she knew something had to be done. She enjoyed being the bully and loved her role that removed her from the daily work. Hiltlin had lusted for the pampered life of their former feudal master. She would not surrender that, and she would defend it at all costs, but she thought the two witches should pay that cost.

Liz and Anya had spent a month in the village, and the grain harvest began under pleasant weather. Children gathered the flax seed heads into a barn, pulled the stalks from the ground and laid them flat to ret in the field. Many adults used small sickles to cut wheat, oats, and barley. They left the large turnip field to provide food for the pigs to rut out on their own.

While Jewel had a constant climate, the weather had random fluctuations as found on any planet where water comprised most of the surface. The oceans of jewel held huge amounts of heat and generated intense storms. While nothing matched an Earth hurricane, and the village lay somewhat inland, streams of wind and rain could happen.

The Miigis saw no reason to interfere with these natural processes on the non-Oshki continents and let their test subjects react in uncontrolled ways. The experiment wanted to test human possibilities, and Earth had a dynamic climate and geology. On Earth, humans had unbalanced the climate. On Jewel, they could not, but the planet, while keeping the Oshki in the ideal, allowed challenges on continents two and three. Such a test visited a disaster in the quiet village. Not even Anya knew if the turn in the weather came from some deliberate new action or was simply how the Miigis had created the experimental places.

The grain harvest had reached the half-way point when the rain came. The crops could stand a normal wet day, but the rain poured down and would not stop. In the three days of the deluge, most of the fields flooded, house roofs leaked and misery held sway. Anya and Liz stayed warm and dry in their tight cottage, but the rude, hand-built village could not hold. Gales littered the yards with thatch and other debris, and the forest surrounding the snug cottage moaned through the nights.

When the sun finally ended the onslaught, the grain lay flat and ruined. The turnip field had become a muddy morass and everyone was damp and depressed. The villagers had seen this before. Disaster loomed. There would be hunger until the next crops matured, and that meant half a year. In the days of the Lord of the land, there might have been some help from above, but that had ended.

"We were better off with the Lord," some villagers lamented and a few more turned to support Hiltlin.

"What," another said. "In the worst times, he stole what little we had. He suffered too and only looked after his own gut. We were only as valuable as his cattle."

As normal, disaster created a situation that brought out the best in some people and ugly selfishness in others. Both hope and danger lurked in disaster.

They searched for explanations and blame. Did God get angry at the village? What did they do wrong? Who was the sinner?

The solution would solve two problems for Hiltlin. She saw Anya as a potential rival and the disaster weakened her authority because it had weakened the bodies and spirits of her villagers. She needed a distraction to rebuild her influence and the witches of the woods would provide it.

The villagers saw that Anya and Liz lived comfortably. Resentment and envy served Hilton's purpose and her strength grew.

"The witches are to blame. They cast a spell on us," Hiltlin shouted to a group in the square. "We must kill them."

"Kill them," echoed from the crowd. Hiltlin's support, even though large, comprised only a third of the village, but it certainly could commit mayhem and murder.

Anya and Liz had visited the village often to help with the salvage of the residue of the crops. The recovering wounded men still needed Anya's help, and she realized that in a hungry time, some might die. Her doctoring separated her from Liz, who laboured in the barn, helping to winnow and dry salvaged grain. It was one of the few times the women had separated.

Liz laboured over a table where they had laid grain brought in from the yard after drying in the sun. The gloomy space reeked of must and dust. Liz wore a scarf over her nose and mouth, as did the women with her. The growing shouts of an angry crowd filtered into the barn. The mob drew closer.

"Forswlen wal-kirie; burn the witch."

Louder, closer...

"Forswlen wal-kirie; forswlen wal-kirie; forswlen wal-kirie..."

The chants grew louder.

Liz frantically searched for a way out. The barn had only one entrance, and the mob had entered the yard.

"Forswlen wal-kirie; forswlen wal-kirie; forswlen wal-kirie..."

The cries echoed from the walls.

"Anya," Liz cried. "Anya..."

Anya did not hear Liz' voice, but she felt her anguish. She raced towards her love. The muddy path tried to slow her, but Anya lifted into the air.

Hurry, she thought, *hurry...*

"Forswlen wal-kirie; forswlen wal-kirie; forswlen wal-kirie..."

Anya could hear the cries. She felt the hate.

The mob surged towards the barn door.

"Come oute," the mob shouted.

"Forswlen wal-kirie; forswlen wal-kirie; forswlen wal-kirie..."

Liz cowered against the rear wall. The four village women with her rushed to the doorway.

"N-wei, n-wei, n-wei," they shouted.

Anya sailed towards the trouble. Suddenly, the air moves of an Oshki game seemed helpful. Tears streamed down her face. Liz had saved her life. She needed to save Liz.

The mob reached the doorway.

"Forswlen wal-kirie; forswlen wal-kirie; forswlen wal-kirie...kill the witch; kill the witch; kill the witch..."

Liz tore frantically at the rear wall. Chunks of dry mud broke off in her hands. If it had been an Earth bank barn, she would easily kick away a board to make her escape. Here, the walls of the crude barn comprised wattle and mud. Given time, the woven mat would yield, but Liz had no time.

"N-wei, n-wei, n-wei,"

The four women stood firm against the mob. They brandished winnowing sticks and menaced the horde.

Anya tried to fly faster.

The commotion had attracted people from other tasks. Women hurried from the gardens and a few men not cutting wood appeared.

"Forswlen wal-kirie," Hiltlin shouted. "Kill the black-faced witch."

"N-wei, n-wei, n-wei," the four brandished their feeble weapons. They tried not to show their fear. Their bravery froze the mob. Some of those crying for blood were relatives of the four heroes. Liz hid deep in the shadows. Anya now saw the barnyard, and felt Liz' fear.

The other crowd of villagers rushing to the sounds became a mass of fury. Most of the villagers saw Hiltlin as a self-serving bully. None were immune to believing in witches, but they believed that if Anya and Liz were witches, they were good ones of God, not the devil. The recovering wounded men told of that. Liz and Anya's burnished and black faces meant God had rescued them from Satan for a special purpose. They were God's angels. The devil would never have eased the suffering of the wounded men.

"N-wei, n-wei, n-wei," the voices of the rushing villagers joined the four brave ones in the barn.

"Forswlen wal-kirie," Hiltlin shouted.

"N-wei, n-wei, n-wei," became urgent cries from the onrushing villagers. The mass outnumbered Hiltlin's mob, and it shrank towards the far fence.

The bulk of villagers swept into the barnyard. Hiltlin's hunters became the prey. A line of saviours rushed between the would-be killers and joined the four brave hearts at the door. Someone threw a clod of clay towards Hiltlin. Another flew. The air filled with flying missiles. People staggered with the effects; some fell to their knees and risked being crushed. Cries of pain joined the angry screams. Never had the village seen such a riot within.

The weaker of Hiltlin's followers rushed to join the new mob. Her inner guard faltered as the onslaught intensified. Bodies pressed on bodies and Hiltlin's group compressed towards the leader.

"Exilen, exilen Hiltlin, exilen gettour, ban the bully."

The village had never been so divided.

The crowd pressed. Hiltlin collapsed in horror. Her game of being dictator ended in fear and loss. Her formerly brave defenders evaporated into the mix. In their attempts to save themselves, they became some of the more vocal, demanding vengeance.

"Drepen, drepen, drepen, kill, kill, kill. "

Some raised the cudgels they had brought to beat Liz and threatened the cowering Hiltlin. The mob of saviours seemed as blood-thirsty as the mob of killers.

Anya arrived, settling unnoticed behind the mob.

"No, no, no," she cried and hurried into the mob.

The mass of women parted in deference to the copper-faced visitor, the healer. Anya finally reached the stricken Hiltlin. She reached down and took her hand to raise a horrified Hiltlin to her feet. Anya turned to the quietened mass of villagers.

"You are missing many men," she cried out. "You need all the hands for the work. Hiltlin is one. Embrace her, love her, save her. She can be of you, not above you. Your strength is your togetherness. Don't choose to fracture that here. Liz and I will soon be gone. Your misfortune with the weather will pass, and you will prosper in both things and happiness."

Liz emerged from the barn. Her trembles had stopped, and the villagers shouted in glee. She reached Anya; stood on the other side of Hiltlin and took her hand. Hiltlin's face still held horror, whether from her near death or from being touched by those she believed to be witches. She feared some magic, some painful death. Hiltlin could not accept that these two witches might love her.

Hiltlin actually believed the two were sorceresses, and she had seen them as evil rivals and handy scape-goats for the bad times that threatened her leadership. Now that her power was forfeit, she only needed to hope for redemption. Hiltlin had resigned to a probable future of lonely exile, or worse. Now, these strange women, witches but wonders of the woods offered her more, with no condemnation or rancour, but some deeper empathy.

"Despite your hardships, you have a bright future. Don't stain it with the memory of violence." Liz said to the crowd. "Take your journey with forgiveness and healing."

Liz would soon return to Earth. She did not realize the irony of her using them on Jewel and the usefulness these words would have when she reached home. She had never thought of Liz Davis as being a proselytizer for peace and an advocate for the mass of suffering humanity. Here, in this moment, Liz simply wanted to save a life.

The crowd had wanted blood. The words of the strangers confused them and then encouraged. They could not afford to lose useful hands, and they knew from the bitter times fighting for the old lord that once blood spilt, it begged for vengeance. Hiltlin had a large family and punishing her would lead to hate. In the immediate crisis, and in their hoped for future, peace would confirm hope.

Rumbling exchanges swept the crowd. The second woman, who had greeted the strangers weeks before, stood beside Anya.

"My friends," she said, "the strangers speak truth. What say ye?"

The villagers had no stomach for fighting and death, and the men recovering from battle wounds in many houses strengthened that, and the weather disaster had exhausted them. They shouted.

"Milcen, milcen, milcen, forgive, forgive, forgive..."

Anya smiled; Liz released a deep breath. Hiltlin cried.

"Ambition should be made of sterner stuff." Liz quoted. She had not fully recovered from the terror of a few minutes ago. Never in her field work had she ever been in actual danger.

Despite her later arrival, Anya knew that her love had never been in real danger. If all else had failed, they would have vanished together in a quantum deception. Magic would not have helped the villagers and would have confirmed the charge of witchcraft. Anya allowed the villagers to intervene to permit healing. Any magic would have led to more fearful superstition and perhaps an ugly civil war.

It took Anya another week to prepare her medical patients for her departure. She used subtle mental adjustments to ease lingering pain. Anya could not restore the two amputated limbs. That would have again raised the spectre of magic, but she showed how they could attach functional prosthetics. Peg legs and hand-hooks were within the ability of the village. These would turn potential burdens into useful members of the village.

The time of departure came. The village, in the hard times, could not afford a feast, and the women decided they would slip away. To avoid legends, they had the children see them carry bundles and disappear into the woods. That would lead to enough myth, but no hint of magic. Liz hoped she might return one day to discover where the legend of the witches of the woods would have gone.

They had expected to be taken into a Species 2 ship once they had gone deeper into the forest, but Mater came to them in a clear mental message.

"Walk east to the sea," Mater said.

Liz and Anya followed the mother's direction. The land sloped gently in the right way, and soon the trees thinned into a broad meadow, swept by sea winds. A path took them down a steep cliff to a cozy inlet.

Liz ran a hand over the rough rocky wall along the path.

"Look," she said, "this is nothing like the Crystal Mountains, nothing like Jewel. This seems to be granite and well weathered."

"The Miigis have great power," Anya said. "Jewel is much more than we Oshki ever knew."

A screaming sea-bird burst from a nesting nook above Liz' head and its cries faded on the breeze.

They reached a narrow strip of sand lapped by warm, gentle wavelets. A catamaran with a full cabin, much larger than the flimsy craft that had betrayed them at the Crystal Mountains, rocked gently in the water.

"Come my love," Anya took Liz' hand. Mater says it is safe and will take us home."

"But we don't know what way or how to sail," Liz said.

"No," Anya said, "but the boat does."

> *The owl and the pussy cat went to sea*
> *In a beautiful pea-green boat*

They climbed aboard and used poles to push away from the beach. An off-shore breeze rose and along with it, the jib sail. The craft and two nervous but happy women were at sea. More sails set without Liz and Anya involved and the boat rose high barely to skim the surface and they sped to the east.

"The Oshki are five days beyond the sea," Anya waved an arm over the sparkling waters and felt happiness.

"It's our honeymoon," Liz said, and she hummed.

> *They danced by the light of the moon*

Chapter 21

From beyond the sea and sky,

Although Liz and Anya's arrival in the land of the Oshki did not resemble that of returning heroes with bands playing and loud cheers, a throng, perhaps the whole of the local Oshki, Ted, Siglinde, Lila and Robert Orville plus the two recognizable Species 2 residents had gathered on the beach. Liz and Anya returned to the spot from where they had first left on their horrible, happy journey to the Crystal Mountains.

The boat crunched onto the sand, and Pater waded into the gentle surf to help the women ashore. He hugged the pair, followed by Mater and the gathering erupted into more emotion, with the Oshki playing an elaborate soaring game above the sand, as the Earthlings smiled in happiness.

The spectacle stunned Lila and Robert Orville. They had experienced Species 2 technology and wonders, but they had never seen the Oshki displaying their abilities before.

"Y'all would think the whole damned universe is magic." Lila said.

"We can't linger," Pater said. "Yours is not the only happy arrival this day."

The throng hurried through the forest towards the landing zone. They found it in meadow glory, but, Siglinde thought, more elaborate and happy than the one when she had arrived. Jewel had put on its equivalent of the red carpet. In fact, it was a yellow carpet, as a wide swath of dandelions extended from the meadow's edge towards a spot in the middle distance.

Siglinde stared at the Earth flowers.

Dandelions?

"I think I know who we are expecting," Siglinde said.

Ted hugged her. He already knew.

Pater held them at the edge, glanced skyward and then to Mater.

She comes... they shared the thought.

The gathering quietly stood, sensing the significance that Mater and Pater gave to the event. Since this was the landing zone, everyone stared skyward. The blue remained unbroken; it seemed forever. Then...

Near the horizon, a speck dropped from the sky. The distance revealed nothing. Slowly, Liz would later write "majestically" in her field notes. The thing grew larger, nearer. It remained coal black against the shimmering sky. As it neared, an imperceptible rumble grew.

The thing became a massive shape, neither round nor square, but a distorted oval. The craft had the dead-black surface of a Miigis ship except as it banked slightly, the reflective surface of the sun-side flashed brilliance from Sigma D. The growl became visceral as it resonated in Siglinde. She had never seen a ship so large. Only Mater and Pater had seen its sister. This one was new, special even to the Oshki ancient ones, the pinnacle of Miigis technology. In fact, they had built their first trans-galactic ship designed to make a journey never before attempted. It had come from the Sagittarian sector, the homeland in the void, via Earth, and bore the happiest and, for the galaxy, the most valuable cargo of all.

It eased to rest, filling the vast meadow and leaving the flowers to dance in shadowed greeting. A slow rotation brought a nub end of the oval near and then it stopped. A port opened exactly above the carpet of yellow. The crowd stepped forward in anticipation and followed the much-shortened dandelion path towards the ship.

No blue or purple light appeared and they hovered close to the ground. Jewel's atmosphere required no protection. A member of Species 2 left the port, eased to the ground and stood before the Oshki. Then a Miigis descended, different from the Species 2, but they stood as equals. Soon, two young women, humans by appearance, stood beside the star travellers. The gathering stared in stunned silence. Not even the Oshki understood.

Siglinde, Ted and Liz smiled. The lack of pomp and ceremony reflected the heart of the younger of the two human females. Star travelling species did not give any honours in their egalitarian culture, but this girl saw herself as a youngster, a learner, ignorant, but also she knew she held an importance that exceeded all others. It had earned her no arrogance; she was simply herself, but a child of the galaxy. It already appeared not to be an honour but threatened to be a burden. The galaxy required no champion, but wisdom would suffice. This hybrid human teenage woman would hold that understanding.

Mater stepped forward, nodded to the Species 2 and the Miigis arrivals, and turned to the human women.

"Welcome, RoH. Welcome dear child of the stars." Mater's voice faltered, as if awe or respect had overwhelmed the wise one.

RoH smiled and stepped to embrace Mater. Mater changed, and so that RoH embraced a Miigis Mater. Every onlooker gasped. Pater joined them as Miigis. They signalled to the arrived Miigis and again, Mater turned to RoH.

"Who is this friend, child?" Mater looked at the other human.

"This is Jaden, my sister, my best friend. She is special, not only to me but to all."

RoH beckoned Siglinde. They embraced.

"I once led you to a high cliff of doubt and fear," RoH said, "but Siglinde, you stepped off that terrifying cliff and you are now free to fly. Earth needs you. There is much for me to tell you, but you will be the one who helps my mother, you, Ted, Liz, and Anya. You gave me strength to fly from my cliff of fear and doubt. Thank you."

"Anya," RoH said to the stunned Oshki woman. "You will travel to Earth with your love. It is the land of your ancestors. They need and welcome you."

RoH touched the recently released Species 2 hermit of the Crystal Mountains.

"Father," RoH said, "I know you knew of me, of my adventures. For most of it, I thought it was you on the ship. But no..."

Briefly, RoH's eyes teared. At this instant, she revealed why the Miigis held her so dear. Her heart felt loved, cared, and sought. She loved humans, Species 2 and Miigis. RoH understood that love, her type of caring for each other, had to enter the hearts of all species, human, Species 2 and Miigis. It must also reach whoever lived in that star system that approached from Andromeda. Even in this sunlit meadow of Jewel, RoH shuddered at the enormity and uncertainty of that arrival. She had not simply stepped from a high cliff; she had stepped into the void.

"I had one father on the ship." RoH turned to the Miigis who accompanied her. "I only learned lately that the truth is I have two fathers. With Robert's father," RoH nodded to the frail species 2, who stood with Lila and Robert, "this seems like Father's Day on Jewel.

"I was going to get you all ugly ties, but I don't know your neck sizes." RoH smirked.

Lila, Liz and Siglinde giggled with RoH. No one else understood the joke.

"The RoH Show has come to Jewel," RoH's Miigis father said, but he did not really understand either. He just knew from her Earthly adventures that RoH did and said the oddest things.

RoH knelt and gently took a dandelion in her fingers. She stroked its leaves, touched the flower and stood.

"No, I am RoH, Species 2, human, and Miigis, and star dust, but I'm still RoH. I'm hungry. Can we have breakfast?"

"Are you a saviour, yet hungry?" Liz asked. Jaden's giggle washed over them.

"Me too," she said.

Mater and Pater reverted to their Oshki human forms and led the way into the trees. RoH's great grandfather and her Miigis father trailed behind. Neither had known what RoH would say. She surprised them, along with the rest of this strange mix of galactic species. On the ship, RoH had mostly sat in quiet thought, or laughed and chatted with Jaden or listened. No alien knew, no one understood, yet all who travelled with RoH on that ship felt contentment and hope.

In the brief time of the arrival, a dwelling had appeared between that of Liz and Siglinde. Nothing on the planet Jewel could surprise the two human scientists. They were sure of their uncertainty about what might happen next. At least, now they understood how the Miigis had created it, and the power that the existence of Jewel implied. On Earth, working for NAAP, Species 2 had awed and frightened them, until they met Ellie. The power of the Miigis dwarfed Species 2, and it left awe in Siglinde, but not the fear.

Siglinde looked at RoH, whose enigmatic smile and joyful fascination over everything stunned her. If the Miigis who walked with RoH had showed facial expressions, Siglinde would have seen one that mimicked her awe and puzzlement. Siglinde wondered if RoH understood RoH. Certainly, no other being in the galaxy seemed capable of it. Siglinde remembered the day she and RoH had met in Charlie Keys' kitchen. She had felt the specialness of RoH then. As they walked, Siglinde watched RoH's taking it all in and RoH's humble thrall at everything new. She had matured since that first time. RoH stood taller and showed all the outward signs of a girl becoming a woman. If possible, her eyes betrayed more confidence than Siglinde remembered at Charlie Keys' table.

How can RoH be so special? Siglinde wondered.

RoH caught Siglinde's stare. She smiled at her human friend and winked.

All will be fine. The thought entered Siglinde's head. *This is a branching of the ways. Once you have been here long enough, you and Liz must return to Earth and lead towards the stars. I must go to the stars, to one specific star to meet and greet those I hope are cousins to us all. It is not sure, but one day, I hope we meet again. Earth is at a dangerous time, but I guarantee you will be safe and everyone you love. The Earth is now in a cocoon of uncertainty. We won't know until we open that chrysalis if humanity lives or dies. Be brave, Siglinde. You must be one of those who opens the cover and sees. I hope with all my heart that humans choose life.*

I want to return with Ted. What do you mean for me to remain on Jewel long enough? Siglinde thought in return. Both RoH's thoughts and her ability to reply in thought stunned Siglinde.

Jewel has already taken you further in your ability. Soon it will be enough. RoH silently replied.

A sudden disruption came from Siglinde and Ted's cottage. A large dog, a yellow Labrador, bound out of the doorway and ran to RoH.

RoH knelt on the soft needle covered ground, welcomed the animal with open arms and accepted sloppy kisses. She looked up at Siglinde.

Thank you RoH thought.

RoH smiled at Art, who had hurried behind, holding a leash. "Who let the dog out?"

Siglinde laughed. She had told Art the day after she had arrived that the Oshki had him on a short leash and had told him they needed dogs on Jewel.

"His name is Jas. He will guide me like Jas did on Earth and travel with me forever."

RoH led the group inside. Only Jaden felt surprise. The interior duplicated the main living area of the old farmhouse near Goderich. None of the others had ever visited the place. The main difference from the farm, a large round table filled what would have been the dining area before the CIA had gutted the place. A robotic server waited near the kitchen door.

"Let's eat," RoH said. She took Jaden's hand, and they sat side by side. Jas curled up at their feet beneath the table. A round table had no head. The others seemed to make RoH's place have that honour, but she would have none of it.

"Will you lead the discussion later?" RoH asked Mater and Pater. "But let's eat first. I recommend eggs, Sigma D up." RoH giggled. "On Earth they would be called sunny side up."

Jaden groaned, RoH chuckled, and Ted and the humans smiled. The aliens remained impassive.

RoH laughed at both her alien fathers.

"I'll get your funny bone yet," she said.

The aliens raised their hands in a gesture of defeat.

Progress, she thought.

The robotic server brought the food, and RoH made sure the machine served her last. The group understood the gesture. RoH, the one they respected the most of all the sentient beings in the galaxy, had told them she would lead by example. To be first was to be last. Her empathy and sense of equity set the standard. While others might revere her, RoH understood that after it all, she could only be one of all living things. Humility, not honour, had to dominate.

The humans and Ted dug into what RoH called a "Texas breakfast" and they tried not to look at whatever the aliens had in front of them. Mater and Pater ate their usual Jewel concoction.

"Y'all going to get me a grill and a pantry," Lila said. "I love to cook."

RoH smirked over a cup of cocoa and then frowned.

She had found the first serious thing that she had to have changed in the galaxy. They needed to learn how to make real Earth hot chocolate.

"Pater," RoH said, "I have to update your food factory template for chocolate. We need to send someone to get real Earth chocolate."

An outside observer might have mistaken breakfast for a galactic diplomatic conference. RoH and the Miigis knew that not to be true. The peaceful galactic diaspora required no negotiations. They did not have any reason to discuss the next steps. RoH knew from her learning on the Miigis ship she would soon leave for the edge of the galaxy. The journey would require at least two Earth years and probably more if they found success. Her quest held hope and uncertainty. If she succeeded, then she would return. It would depend on events on Earth if she returned there or to Jewel.

RoH set her mug on the table and examined Liz and Anya. Their minds contained their recent adventures and their love. RoH was most interested in their stay in the village. She turned to Mater and Pater.

"The experiment of Jewel must end," she said. Although it was not, it seemed to be an order.

"We already decided," Mater said. "You see that in the recent experience of Anya and Liz. We have learned all we needed there, and now all on Jewel can live their lives and we hope they have happy futures. We will still watch and not allow any horrors."

"We owe it to those people," RoH said. Her inclusive words said that she accepted some responsibility. While the Miigis experiment of Jewel had not been a mistake or a failure, it represented the reality that in the galaxy, blame did not factor.

Learning from mistakes and progress from that learning were all that mattered. Learning human empathy would give moral guidance.

"We will soon go our separate ways." RoH said.

"Jewel must be attended to," RoH looked at Mater.

"Earth must be saved," she said. Her eyes swept over the humans, Anya and Ted. It seemed obvious what their task would be.

"Jaden, my dearest friend, you must remain on Jewel to learn and grow."

Jaden sobbed.

"Jaden," Anya said and slid close to the Earth girl.

Anya used her palm to stroke Jaden's head and hair. Jaden calmed.

"You are pure human," Anya said, "but you are different. The galaxy needs you.

"Welcome, dear, welcome to the universe."

"Jaden," RoH hugged her. "Your brain will change here. You will learn from the Oshki and Jewel will change you. If I succeed, you will be necessary in the galaxy's future. You will help complete my work, and you will have your own. That lies in the future. For now, Jewel must be home. It is simply a step on the hill we climb together. When I return, Jewel will be my first stop, and we will be together again, friends once more and forever.

"Of course," RoH rubbed Jas behind the ear, "you will have to get your own dog."

"I'm afraid," Jaden said. "I'm homesick already. What about Mom and Dad and my dorky brother? What about Grandma Emily?"

RoH paused, looked at her empty chocolate mug, and then at her Miigis father. She smiled, and Jaden knew something mischievous would happen.

"You will make a quick return trip to Earth. Jaden, visit your family and assure them you will be back. They can reach you through the farm.

"Ask Emily to come to Jewel with you. I once promised to take her on a trip to the stars. She will come. She will love to chat with these two old fogies."

RoH nodded at Mater and Pater.

"More importantly," RoH giggled, "you will buy me all the chocolate powder I need. I will wait here for your return. Remember, I joked once that your job was to make me happy. This will make me happy as it makes you happy.

"Anya and Liz, you soon will return to Earth to help Ellie try to show humans the way to survive. You will spend time with Dawn Waasnodae and Liz Dafoe and the Anishinaabe. They and their like around the planet is the key. Anya, you descend from them, and Liz will love the field study. Combining the ancient solutions of the tribes with galactic understanding will offer an example to humanity."

"What will I do?" Siglinde asked.

"Your job," RoH said. "Help humans untangle the quantum riddle. Hopefully, my mother and others will buy you the time to do that. I understand the plan is for you to hide out on the farm near Goderich. Don't let Elsie and Jake annoy you too much, and Captain Fontaine loves chess.

"All of that is important," RoH said, "but this is my new purpose."

"What," Siglinde asked.

An image of a star system appeared in Siglinde's mind. It hung in coal-black space.

"That is a rogue system that left Andromeda millions of Earth years ago and is now entering our galaxy. It is my destination."

"When do you leave?" Siglinde asked.

"Soon, Siglinde," said RoH, "as soon as Jaden returns here. I need to get a shipment of cocoa from Earth, and you need to go home. You will also reach the stars."

RoH flashed an enigmatic smile of anticipation, uncertainty, and hope.